The Final Bow

I shut the door to the costume room, stopping the cold wind. Because the room was so neat and organized, my eye caught a black shoe overturned under a clothing rack. I crouched and grabbed it with the intention of setting it with the others, but it wouldn't move—because there was a foot in it.

I was tempted to shut my eyes but forced them to stay open as I wheeled the rack away from the wall. It was Harry Schrumm, *Knock 'Em Dead*'s producer.

He was slumped against the wall, a round circle of blood oozing around the knife in his chest. His eyes were open; he was looking directly at me, as if asking for help.

Too late for that.

Other *Murder, She Wrote* mysteries

Knock 'Em Dead

A *Murder, She Wrote* Mystery

A Novel by Jessica Fletcher
and Donald Bain
based on the
Universal television series
created by Peter S. Fischer,
Richard Levinson & William Link

A SIGNET BOOK

SIGNET
Published by New American Library, a division of
Penguin Putnam Inc., 375 Hudson Street,
New York, New York 10014, U.S.A.
Penguin Books Ltd, 27 Wrights Lane,
London W8 5TZ, England
Penguin Books Australia Ltd, Ringwood,
Victoria, Australia
Penguin Books Canada Ltd, 10 Alcorn Avenue,
Toronto, Ontario, Canada M4V 3B2
Penguin Books (N.Z.) Ltd, 182–190 Wairau Road,
Auckland 10, New Zealand

Penguin Books Ltd, Registered Offices:
Harmondsworth, Middlesex, England

First published by Signet, an imprint of New American Library,
a division of Penguin Putnam Inc.

First Printing, October 1999
10 9 8 7 6 5 4 3 2 1

PUBLISHER'S NOTE
This is a work of fiction. Names, characters, places, and incidents either are
the product of the author's imagination or are used fictiously, and any
resemblance to actual persons, living or dead, events, or locales is entirely
coincidental.

For my mother and father,
who believed in me.

Preface

A Summer Day in Cabot Cove

"What's new in that city you call home?" Dr. Seth Hazlitt asked my publisher, Vaughan Buckley, and his wife, Olga. They'd taken a week that summer to drive through New England and had stopped for lunch in Cabot Cove.

"Hot and humid," Olga said. "Nothing new."

"I was pleased to read that the murder rate in New York is down," I said as we sat in Mara's dockside restaurant enjoying her rich, thick New England clam chowder and home baked bread.

"It'll start going up again if they don't catch that Broadway serial killer," Vaughan said, pouring the remains of a chilled bottle of California sauvignon blanc into our glasses.

"Broadway serial killer?" I said. "I hadn't heard about that."

"It'll probably hit the national press," Olga said, "now that he's taken his third victim."

"It's a man?" Seth asked.

"A sexist assumption on my part," she said.

"Three murders?" I said. "Why do you call him, or her, the *Broadway* serial killer?"

"Because all three killings have taken place backstage in Broadway theaters," Vaughan explained. "First a young actress, then a middle-aged actor. The one just as we were leaving the city involved an up-and-coming director. All very bizarre in the way they're carried out. He—I have to assume it's a man—always leaves a calling card of sorts that reflects the play with which the victims are involved."

"The middle-aged actor was doing Shakespeare," Olga said. "He was stabbed to death in his dressing room wearing only underwear, according to what I read. But the killer took the time to place the headpiece the actor wore in the show on his head." She turned to Vaughan. "What did he do with the actress?"

"Posed her with a martini glass in her hand and a cigarette dangling from her lips. She was playing a high-priced prostitute."

"Any leads?" I asked.

2

"Evidently not," Vaughan said, "at least not any the police have reported."

"I'm surprised more of it doesn't happen in theaters," Seth said, sitting back and dabbing at his mouth with a napkin.

We looked at him.

"What do you mean by that?" I asked.

"Well, it seems to me that in order to be an actor or actress, you have to be a little . . . strange."

We laughed.

"I take it from your comment that you think the Broadway killer is an actor or actress," Olga said.

"*Ayuh*. Makes sense. Actors and actresses live in their own little fantasy world. They have to be playing other characters all the time instead of being themselves."

Vaughan glanced at me and smiled.

"Maybe Seth has a point," I said defensively. "Actors and actresses would have access to backstage areas. And, their sense of the dramatic could fuel a need to use props on the deceased."

We dropped the subject, finished our lunch, and the Buckleys spent a few hours at my house before heading off for an inn a hundred miles up the coast.

"Wish you could stay a while," I said, kissing them on their cheeks.

"Maybe another time, Jess," said Vaughan. "I

hope the talk about the Broadway serial killer hasn't upset you."

My laugh was not entirely genuine. The truth was, it *had* upset me. "Of course not," I said. "After all, I write murder mysteries."

"Maybe your next one will be about killers on Broadway," Olga said.

"I don't think so," I said. "Broadway is furthest from my mind as a setting for murder. Drive carefully, and stop in on your way back if you have time."

I watched them leave my driveway, waved, and went inside for a cup of tea. Visions of the murder victims as described kept flashing in front of me.

Whoever is doing the killing on Broadway must be a very sick individual, I thought. The whistling tea kettle broke my reverie, and those grotesque images disappeared in the bracing aroma of the tea and happy contemplation of what was left of the day.

Chapter 1

"Bravo!"

We jumped to our feet and applauded as the conductor of Cabot Cove's symphony orchestra, Peter Eder, took his bows after leading the ensemble through Benjamin Britten's "Four Sea Interludes" from the opera, *Peter Grimes*. It was the final in a summer series of concerts. Labor Day was only days away.

Dr. Seth Hazlitt leaned over to me and said, "Peter is truly amazing, what he can coax from the orchestra."

"He's our gain, Connecticut's loss," I said.

That the small town of Cabot Cove had a symphony orchestra at all was remarkable, and to have lured Peter Eder from where he'd been musi-

5

cal director and conductor for the Connecticut Symphony Orchestra only enhanced the experience.

The decision to fund an orchestra came after months of heated debate within the town council. The mayor, Jim Shevlin, was firmly committed to the undertaking. Others on the council considered it folly. Our chamber of commerce tipped the scale in favor of it. Its president, Tony Colarusso, eloquently stated at the pivotal meeting: "Summer tourism in this area is on the upswing, and we have an obligation to provide more than lobster bakes, sandy beaches, and salt water taffy. An orchestra will draw from all the surrounding communities and bring money into Cabot Cove. Tourism will increase, our citizens will benefit from having a rich musical resource in its midst, and Cabot Cove will gain a reputation as a coastal cultural haven." He presented the council members with a petition supporting an orchestra signed by every member of the chamber.

Actually, launching the orchestra and bringing Peter Eder to town were only part of a cultural boom in that area of Maine, which includes Cabot Cove. Our regional theater had become more adventuresome in the plays it chose to perform, and a writer's retreat had opened, wooing some impressive names for its faculty from New York City.

Seth drove me home after the cocktail party celebrating the evening's performance, the last of the concert season, and came in for a nightcap.

"Exciting things happening in Cabot Cove these days," he said, settling into his favorite recliner in my study and tasting brandy from a balloon snifter.

"Yes, and I love every minute of it. Oh, by the way, the tickets arrived this afternoon." I retrieved an envelope from my desk and handed it to him. The return address read "Theatre Direct International." Seth opened it and perused its contents—dozens of tickets to shows on Broadway and London's West End. A member of the chamber of commerce, Susan Shevlin, wife of our mayor and owner of the town's leading travel agency, had put together a package that included flying to London to catch shows there, and then to New York to do the same. Our tickets on British Air from Boston to London, and London to New York, had arrived a few days earlier. We were scheduled to leave in a week.

"Looks as though everything's in order, Jessica. Wouldn't expect any less from Susan. How many did we end up with?"

"Fourteen, counting you and me."

"A fair turnout. I suspect you'll be seeing your friend while in London, Inspector Sutherland."

I smiled and said, "Of course. We'll only be

there a few days, most of which will be spent in theaters. But I'll find some time for George."

I'd met Scotland Yard Inspector George Sutherland in London years ago while attending a mystery writers' conference. A dear friend, Marjorie Ainsworth, the reigning queen of mystery writers, was stabbed to death in her country manor home outside London, and George Sutherland was assigned the case. We had become close friends since then, bordering on the romantic. I stress the term "bordering"—ours was a platonic mutual admiration society.

"Another brandy?" I asked.

"Thank you, no, Jessica. I'd best be going." Seth went to the door, paused, turned, and asked, "No one's ever adapted one of your books into a stage play, have they?"

"No. Matt Miller came close a few times in selling stage rights, but the deals fell through at the last minute." Matt was my literary agent.

"Your new one, *Knock 'Em Dead*, would make a fine play."

"Yes, it would. I'll bring that up with Matt the next time we speak. I'll be seeing him when we're in New York."

"Good night, Jessica."

"Good night, Seth. See you tomorrow."

I was bubbling with anticipation of the trip. It would be first class all the way, flying on my favorite airline, British Air, and staying in top hotels: the Ritz in London and the Westin Central Park South in New York. I'd stayed there last year when visiting my publisher and fell in love with its European ambiance and sweeping views of Central Park.

But what especially had my juices flowing was the contemplation of spending so much time in theaters. There's something magical about live theater, a visceral experience not delivered by any other medium. I thought about what Seth had said, that none of my many novels had been adapted for the stage. Some movies, yes, but not Broadway, or London's splendid West End. *Knock 'Em Dead*, my most recent mystery novel, had been on the best-seller list for months. Of course, that didn't automatically make it an appropriate vehicle for the stage. But I'd deviated from my usual approach when writing it, confining the action to just a few settings. Too, it was a dialogue-driven book, with intense interaction among characters carrying the story.

A play within a book.

I certainly would raise it with Matt when we hooked up in New York.

Chapter 2

As it turned out, I was able to spend only an hour with George Sutherland in London. He was off to the Cotswolds on a case when we arrived, returning to the city the morning we were to depart for New York. We met for breakfast at the Ritz.

"You're the proverbial sight for sore eyes," he said, joining me at the elaborately set table.

"You look pretty good yourself, George. What sort of case were you on?"

"Too grisly to go into, I'm afraid. One of those nasty domestic disputes that got entirely out of hand. Two people dead, three children orphaned. Enough about that, Jessica. Tell me, what have you been doing in London since you and your friends arrived?"

"Soaking up every bit of theater we can. It's been glorious, a little tiring, but worth every fatiguing minute. We saw *Chicago, Art, Jeckyll and Hyde, Wait Until Dark, The Scarlet Pimpernel*—oh, yes, the highlight was *The Complete Works of William Shakespeare Abridged.* George, it was hilariously funny. And, I sneaked off with my friend, Seth Hazlitt, to see *The Mousetrap* again. It's got to be the fifth or sixth time I've seen it."

"Longest running play in theater history."

"For good reason."

"You look supremely happy, Jessica."

"I am. I walk out of a theater as though I've been transported to some distant place. Then again, that's what good theater is supposed to do to you, isn't it?"

He laughed, causing his handsome, rugged, tanned face to break into a mosaic of creases. "That's what they say. You're going on to New York for more of the same?"

"Yes. I wish I had a few extra days to spend here with you."

"I wish you did, too. Any immediate plans to come back?"

"No, although I can always make such plans. It depends on when Vaughan wants my next book. He's my publisher."

"I know. Tell him for me that he's not to work you too hard, and to leave time for at least a long weekend in London. Will you tell him that?"

I covered his hand on the table with mine and smiled. "Yes, I will tell him that."

"Interesting, Jessica, that when you called to tell me you'd be traveling here on a theater package, my instant thought was that your newest, *Knock 'Em Dead*, would make a wonderful play. I read it while I was away."

"Seth said the same thing, and I've been thinking ever since how much I would enjoy seeing that particular book come to life with live actors and actresses speaking the words I've written, playing out the scenes I've created, and to be able to sit in the theater and see and hear how the audience responds. That's the trouble with writing books. You have no idea who's reading them. More important, there's no sense for the author of how those same people react to what you've written, aside from their letters, of course, but even that doesn't offer the immediacy the stage does. Am I rambling?"

"Yes, and I'm enjoying every word. Why don't you speak with that agent of yours in New York, Miller, is it?"

"Number one on my agenda."

We embraced on the street in front of the hotel.

"Remember now," he said, "you've promised to get back here, and soon."

"Of course I remember. A promise is a promise."

He walked away with purposeful strides, and a lump formed in my throat. I loved being with him, hearing his Scottish brogue, seeing the mischief in his knowing gray eyes, and feeling the calm comfort he always seemed to provide.

The rest of the day was a blur of activity. I sandwiched in a quick visit with my British publisher, had my hair done at a stylish shop in Mayfair, bought a few gifts to bring home, and met my friends at the hotel for the trip to Heathrow Airport and our BA 747 flight across the Atlantic to New York. Seth and I sat next to each other.

"And how is the good Inspector Sutherland?" he asked as the flight attendant served us champagne, caviar, and smoked salmon shortly after takeoff.

"He's fine. Sends his best to you."

"You like him very much, don't you?"

His question surprised me. I'd never made my feelings for George a secret.

"Of course I do. You know that."

"Must be difficult to see him in such short bursts."

I nodded. "Very difficult."

"You should invite him to Cabot Cove."

"Oh, I have, many times. He just never seems to find a chunk of free time to make the trip."

"Well, we'll just have to work on that," Seth said.

"All right, we'll do that," I said, pleased that my dear friend from Cabot Cove felt that way. I sometimes sensed that he disapproved of my relationship with George.

The flight to Kennedy Airport was smooth and uneventful, the ride into the city peaceful. We gathered in the Westin Park Avenue South's lovely lobby and began the check-in process. When it came to me, the young man behind the desk said, "Welcome, Mrs. Fletcher. Good to have you back again."

"My pleasure."

"You have some messages," he said, handing me slips of paper. I quickly perused them. One was from Vaughan Buckley, my publisher, who wanted me to call. A similar message was from my agent, Matt Miller. A few old friends in Manhattan who knew of my travel plans had also left phone numbers.

"Thank you," I said.

"Enjoy your stay."

"I intend to."

We'd landed at 7:40. It was now a little after nine.

"Feel like some dinner?" Seth asked as a bellhop prepared to lead me to my room.

"I don't think so, Seth. I want to return these phone calls, have room service, and get to bed."

"A sensible approach. See you at breakfast."

I unpacked the minute my bags arrived, the first thing I always do when arriving at a hotel, no matter how tired I am. My previous stay at the hotel found me in a room facing the park. This time, I had a stunning view of Manhattan's famous skyline, ablaze with lights and brimming with energy. There's considerable truth to what people say, that New York generates a dynamism not found in any other city in the world. I was energized just looking out over it, my fatigue from the long trip now just a memory.

I sat at a desk, picked up the phone, and started returning the calls, beginning with Matt. I caught him at home.

"Jessica," he said enthusiastically, "great to hear your voice. Just arrive?"

"A little bit ago. How are you?"

"Terrific. I was heading out to grab some dinner. Susan's out of town on business. Join me?"

"I'd planned on staying in the room and ordering something light."

"Absolutely not. I have some wonderful news to share with you."

"Oh? What is it?"

He laughed. "You're not getting off that easy, Jess. No dinner, no news."

"Not fair," I said.

"Who ever said literary agents were supposed to be fair? A half hour?"

"All right. Besides, there was something I wanted to discuss with you."

"What?"

"Two can play your game, Matt. At dinner."

"You're not only talented, you're tough."

"Who ever said writers weren't supposed to be?"

"Tell you what. I've discovered a wonderful Italian restaurant on Fifty-fifth, between Fifth and Sixth. La Vineria. The best southern Italian cooking I've ever tasted. Meet you there? I'd pick you up, but this will be faster."

"All right.

"Fifth-fifth, between Fifth and Sixth?"

"See you there."

Matt was at the restaurant when I arrived after the short walk and we settled at a cozy corner table.

"It's a beautiful room," I said. "I feel like I'm in Italy."

"It is authentic. See that young woman greeting those customers?"

"Yes."

"She's one of the owners, Angela Castaldo. Used to be a top fashion model."

"I can see why. She's beautiful. I have a feeling you come here often."

"As often as I can. This is sort of my table."

"How chic."

"How New York. Drink?"

"Water. Sparkling. So, what's this news you have for me?"

"You first. You said you had something to discuss with me. Mind if I order for both of us?"

"Not at all, but keep it light. I wanted to talk to you about the possibility of selling stage rights to *Knock 'Em Dead*. This trip has really gotten me thinking about the theater and how much I'd love to see one of my works become a play. *Knock 'Em Dead* seems the logical candidate, considering the way it's structured. Don't you agree?"

"What? Oh, sure." He motioned for a waiter and ordered salads and veal marsala for two. To me: "You were saying?"

"I was saying I'd like to see *Knock 'Em Dead* end up on the stage. I—Matt, why do I get the impression you aren't interested in what I'm saying?"

He lifted his glass of red wine in a toast. I picked up my water glass, and we touched rims. "Here's to seeing you again, Jess."

"Matt."

"Yes?"

"Do you think you could interest a producer in mounting a stage production of *Knock 'Em Dead?*"

"Sure."

"*Sure?* You're that confident?"

He nodded, said, "Uh-huh. As confident as this

17

makes me." He reached into his inside jacket pocket, withdrew a paper folded in thirds, and handed it to me.

"What's this?"

"Read it."

I looked at him quizzically as I slowly unfolded the letter. The first three words, in bold letters, came off the page: **Letter of Intent.**

"I don't understand," I said.

"You will if you keep reading."

When I was finished with the four paragraphs, I laid the letter on the table, sat back, cocked my head, narrowed my eyes, and said, "You are a devil."

He grinned broadly. "I am an agent," he said, "which some people think is akin to being Satan. Of course, you aren't among that cynical number."

"No, I am not. When did you make this deal?"

"Wrapped it up this afternoon. The letter is dated today. I wanted to be able to give it to you while you were in New York soaking up Broadway with your friends."

"You're a *sweet* devil."

"Thank you."

"I can't believe this."

"Believe it. Harry Schrumm is the hottest producer on Broadway. No musicals. Strictly drama, the best in town. I sent him *Knock 'Em Dead* a week ago. He read it in one sitting, called me, and said, 'This could be New York's answer to London's *Mousetrap*.' Know what else he said?''

"What?"

"He said, 'She's better than Christie.' "

"Which I'm not, of course, but it was kind of him to say it."

"Never use the word 'kind' when discussing Harry Schrumm. He's a first-class bastard, a really nasty guy. But he has clout, can make things happen—he'll make *this* happen. He wants you to collaborate with a playwright he's chosen to do the adaptation."

"Who is that?"

"I don't know. We'll find out tomorrow night at the party."

"What party?"

"The celebration. At Windows on the World. In your honor. Harry will be there. So will the playwright. And, as an extra added attraction, the actress he's already approached to play Samantha will join us."

"My Samantha? From the book?"

"Right on."

"Matt, I can't go to a party. I have tickets to see—what are we seeing tomorrow night?—oh, *The Beauty Queen of Leenane*. It's supposed to be excellent."

"Eight o'clock curtain?"

"Yes."

"No problem. The party's from six until seventhirty. I'll have a limo take you to the theater."

"There's a matinee tomorrow, too."

"Fine. I'll have the limo take you from the theater to the party."

"This is all somewhat dizzying. Here I was fantasizing about having my book turned into a stage play, and suddenly it's reality."

He poured wine into my empty glass, picked up his glass again, and offered another toast: "To Jessica Fletcher, the new queen of Broadway."

"Oh, my."

"Eat your veal," he said as the waiter delivered our entrees. "It's world class."

Chapter 3

"That's wonderful news," Barbara DePaoli said at breakfast at the hotel the next morning, after I'd announced that *Knock 'Em Dead* would be a Broadway play. Barbara was the secretary of Cabot Cove's chamber of commerce and one of my dearest friends.

"About time," our sheriff, Mort Metzger, said.

"Amen," Mort's wife, Maureen, added.

"They're having a party in your honor at Windows on the World?" Charlene Sassi said, wide-eyed. She owned Cabot Cove's best bakery. "Pretty fancy."

"It's really not in my honor," I said. "It's just to announce that this producer, Harry Schrumm, has optioned the book for the stage."

"Who's going to play Samantha?" Bob Daros, whose Heritage Fuel kept our furnaces going in the winter, asked. "I really liked that character."

"I have no idea," I said. "I'll find out tonight."

Someone had brought that morning's edition of the *Daily News* to the table. The front page headline read: BROADWAY KILLER HITS AGAIN.

"Did you read about this?" Bob asked, holding up the paper for all to see.

"How many does this make?" I asked.

"Four," he answered, "according to the story." He handed me the paper.

"It happened at the Von Feurston Theater," I said, reading aloud. "That's next door to the Drummond Theater, where *Knock 'Em Dead* is scheduled to play."

"This time a producer got it," Charlene said. "He was sixty-three."

The reporter pointed out that when the producer's body was found, a wad of bills was stuffed into his mouth.

"Damn nut," someone said.

Which seemed to sum it up, and ended the conversation about serial killers, at least for that morning.

We saw a play in the afternoon, *Honour*, starring one of my favorite actresses, Jane Alexander. When it let out, we returned to the hotel where most of the group planned to have dinner in its restaurant, Fantino, before heading to an evening performance of *The Beauty Queen of Leenane*.

"Wish you could join us," Mort Metzger said.

"I do, too," I said, "but the limo is picking me up any minute. Hopefully, they'll have something to eat at the party. I'll catch up with you at the theater."

My driver was a placid young man who seemed unfazed by the insanely congested streets leading downtown to the financial district at that hour. We chatted pleasantly until he dropped me off at the entrance to one of two towers comprising the World Trade Center, each soaring a quarter of a mile above lower Manhattan. Views from the 107th floor, where the restaurant, bar, and private rooms were located, were legendary, and I looked forward to enjoying them. In all my trips to New York, I'd never gotten there.

When I stepped off the elevator, Matt Miller and Vaughan Buckley stood waiting. After warm greetings, they escorted me into a handsomely appointed private room with a wall of windows.

"It's breathtaking," I said, looking out over the water and Statue of Liberty.

"Can't beat the view," Vaughan said as a man approached. He was short—I'd say no taller than five feet, five inches—and compactly built. He wore an English-cut blue double-breasted suit, blue-and-white striped shirt with a solid white collar, and red tie. Although he'd gone bald on top, black hair on the side of his head was slicked back, a few strands falling fashionably over his shirt collar. Everything about him said money, power, and ego.

"Harry, meet Jessica Fletcher," Matt said.

"Harry Schrumm," he said, taking my hand. "A pleasure meeting you, Mrs. Fletcher."

"The pleasure is mine, Mr. Schrumm. And please call me Jessica."

"All right. I'm Harry. We're in this for the long run and might as well be comfortable with each other."

A waiter carrying a tray of hot hors d'oeuvres passed, and I plucked a fried oyster to feed my noisy stomach.

"Adapting *Knock 'Em Dead* for the stage won't be easy," Schrumm said. "There are structural problems to overcome."

"Really? I thought the book's structure was part of its appeal as a play. Small setting, lots of dialogue."

Schrumm's smile was patronizing. "You just leave the adaptation to us, Jessica. Writing books is different from writing plays."

"But good storytelling is good storytelling, no matter what the medium," I said, somewhat defensive after his mini-lecture on writing.

Schrumm looked over the crowd that had gathered and waved to someone. We were joined by an older man with flowing gray hair, heavy tortoise shell glasses, and wearing a red-and-yellow checkered shirt with button-down collar, yellow knit tie, brown corduroy jacket with patches at the elbows, jeans, and work boots. A cold pipe was clenched in his teeth.

"Jessica, say hello to Aaron Manley."

We shook hands.

"Aaron has signed on to adapt your book for the stage."

"Wonderful," I said. "You're a playwright?"

"Yes." His inflection said he was surprised I didn't already know it.

"Aaron has a show playing Off-Broadway," Schrumm said. *Revenge of the Honeybadger.*"

"Interesting title," Vaughan said. "I haven't seen it."

"Very profound," Schrumm said.

"A psychological drama," Manley said. "You know, of course, the tendency of the honeybadger when cornered."

Vaughan, Matt, and I looked at each other.

Manley said, "When a honeybadger is cornered, it instinctively attacks the genitals of its enemy."

"Robert Ruark wrote a fine book called *The Honeybadger*," Vaughan said.

"Did he?" Manley said, obviously annoyed that another writer had used the theme before. "I'm not aware of it."

"I understand from Matt that I'll be working with you," I said.

25

"That's to be discussed," Schrumm said. "For now, enjoy the drinks and food. It's costing a damn fortune." He walked away, shoulders squared, stride arrogant, acknowledging comments made to him with a forced smile and wave of his hand. Aaron Manley excused himself and went over to an attractive young woman who had just entered the room. They pressed cheeks, first one, then the other.

Matt whispered to me, "Don't let all this preliminary chitchat get to you, Jess. These theater people can be a little precious at times."

"I have no problem," I said. "I'm still on cloud nine that this is actually going to happen, a book of mine headed for Broadway. It *will* be Broadway, won't it? Not Off-Broadway."

"Absolutely. That's being written into the contract."

"Where's the actress who's to play Samantha?" I asked.

Matt shrugged.

"Who is she?" Vaughan asked.

"No idea," Matt said. "Schrumm told me she'd be here. Kept her name to himself. Schrumm can be very dramatic, very theatrical."

"I'd like to know more about Mr. Manley's background," I said.

"I know a little about him," Vaughan said. "He's been around the New York theater scene for a long time. He had a moderately successful play on Broadway a number of years ago. I can't remember its name. He teaches playwriting at some of the local colleges, made sort of a name for himself in regional theater. He submitted a proposal for a book to us a few years ago, something to do with using acting techniques to find your inner self. A self-help book. We turned it down."

"He *looks* like a playwright," I said.

"Out of central casting," Matt said. "Drink?"

"Sure."

As we stood at the bar, we were approached by an attractive middle-aged couple, dressed for a formal affair later that evening. He wore a tuxedo, she an ankle-length black sheath topped with overtly expensive gold roping, and impossibly high high heels.

"Jessica Fletcher," he said, smiling broadly to reveal very white teeth, made more so by the coppery tan of his face. "I'm Arnold Factor. This is my wife, Jill."

"A pleasure to meet both of you."

"We're very excited about seeing your book turned into a play," she said.

"So am I," I said. "Are you involved with theater in New York?"

"Very much so," he said. "We've backed a number of Harry's plays."

"Really? They say backing Broadway shows is a risky investment. Worse than gambling in Las Vegas or Atlantic City."

"Not if you know what you're doing," Jill said, meaning it. "It's a matter of choosing the right material, the proper creative talent, and keeping close tabs on the way the money is spent."

Arnold laughed. "Which is never easy with Harry," he said, nodding in Schrumm's direction. "Blink and suddenly he's added three alleged cousins to the payroll."

I, too, laughed. "That happens on Broadway, too? I've heard stories about padded payrolls in Hollywood but—"

"Hollywood has nothing on Broadway, especially when Harry Schrumm is involved. He's a good producer, picks good material and pulls together effective creative talent. But—"

"But don't blink," Jill said.

"I'll keep that in mind," I said.

"No, I will," Matt said. "That's what agents are supposed to do, not blink when money is involved."

"We must get together, just the three of us," Jill said, ignoring Matt, "providing the Broadway killer doesn't get us first." She laughed nervously. "I'm anxious to hear the direction you think *Knock 'Em Dead* should take, Jessica."

"I'd enjoy that very much. I understand from Harry I'll be spending a lot of time in New York."

"As you should," Arnold said. "Give us a call next time you're in town." He handed me a card: Factor Enterprises.

"I certainly will," I said.

When it got to be seven-fifteen, I suggested to Matt that I had to leave if I was to meet my friends for the eight o'clock curtain.

"The car's downstairs," he said. "I'll ride uptown with you." To Vaughan: "Need a ride?"

"That would be nice."

I said my good-byes to people I'd met during the party, including the Factors.

"Nothing works on Broadway without big bucks being raised," Matt told me as we watched the Factors make their way to the elevators. "That's really all that Schrumm or any other producer does, raise money."

"Do you think there'll be a problem with that?"

"No. He wouldn't have put up an advance for you if he didn't know he had the money to mount the show. He's too savvy to stick his neck out. Let's go."

We walked to the elevators and Vaughan pushed the "Down" button. The doors suddenly slid open. The only person in the elevator was a woman. We all recognized her.

"Good evening, Ms. Larsen," Vaughan said.

She smiled sweetly, stepped from the elevator, looked at me, and said, "You are Jessica Fletcher, who created that delicious character, Samantha, in *Knock 'Em Dead*."

"Yes," I said. "Are you—?"

"Playing Samantha in the stage production? I believe I am, if it's acceptable to you."

"It's—of course it's acceptable. It's a pleasure meeting you."

I introduced Vaughan and Matt to April Larsen, an actress familiar to most of America. Not that she was a star. She'd been poised on the threshold of Hollywood stardom twenty years ago after making a succession of good films. But then she faded from the upper tier of mega-star actresses—something to do with rumors that her temperamental personality made her a bad risk for big-budget movies.

Although she had not achieved box-office status, she continued to work in lesser films, and with touring companies of Broadway and London shows. She did commercials and had a brief, unsuccessful fling as a TV talk show hostess. What impressed me was that she'd established, and sustained, a relatively positive image throughout her career despite her reputation as being temperamental. She was considered a solid, versatile actress, capable, workmanlike, lending her familiar name to whatever show in which she chose to appear and garnering for the most part solid reviews. It was my impression she hadn't worked much recently.

I meant it when I said it was okay with me if she played my character, Samantha, a woman in her early sixties who, while attempting to keep a dysfunctional family together, finds herself deeply involved in murder within that family. As she attempts to solve the mystery, her own life begins to unravel, to the point where she almost becomes the next victim. Some reviewers of the book said Samantha had a "Tennessee Williams quality to her," which pleased me. Others saw her as a symbol of strength while those around her succumbed to weakness. I'd worked hard to shape Samantha into a three-dimensional, sympathetic woman.

"I'm anxious to sit down and discuss Samantha with you, Jessica."

"I'd love that," I said.

"Not leaving so soon?" she said. "I ran late. Please stay a while."

"Sorry, but I can't. I'm meeting friends at the theater."

"What are you seeing?"

"The Beauty Queen of Leenane."

"A wonderful show. Marie Mullen is superb. The whole cast is. We'll be in touch."

Matt Miller handed her his card. "I'm Jessica's

agent, Ms. Larsen. You can always reach her through me."

"Good. I'll call you once it's set that I'm playing Samantha. Harry assured me I am, but you never know in this business. Lovely meeting you, Mr. Buckley, Mr. Miller. And Mrs. Fletcher, thanks for creating Samantha."

"Nice woman," Vaughan said as we made our way uptown in the limousine. "I always admire performers like her."

"So do I," I said. "I think she'll make a wonderful Samantha."

"I agree," Matt said.

They dropped me at the Walter Kerr Theatre on West Forty-eighth Street where my friends from Cabot Cove milled about on the sidewalk. It was ten minutes to curtain time. I told Vaughan and Matt I'd call the next day, got out, and waved as the limo pulled away.

"How was the party?" Seth asked.

"Quite pleasant. April Larsen is going to play Samantha."

"Didn't know she was still around."

I laughed. "Very much still around, Seth. She looks wonderful and was so gracious. I'm thrilled she'll be doing the part."

I looked up at the marquee where the name of the show, and of cast members, the director, and others were proudly displayed. For a moment, I imagined the marquee went blank. But then it was filled with:

Knock 'Em Dead
Based Upon the Book by Jessica Fletcher
Starring April Larsen
Produced by Harry Schrumm

The only thing missing was the name of the director, because I didn't know it.

"Jessica?" Seth said.

"What?"

"Coming? The show's about to start."

"Oh, yes. I was daydreaming. Yes, let's get inside. I don't want to miss a minute of it."

Chapter 4

Two days after I'd returned to Cabot Cove with my theater-going friends, I received a package in the mail from Matt Miller. In it was the formal agreement between Harry Schrumm's production company and my publisher, Buckley House, as well as papers for me to sign. Matt had cautioned me before I left New York that licensing a book for the stage generally meant a small amount of money up front. This agreement was no exception. If money were to be made, it would come later, after the play had opened and had generated enough in ticket sales to show a profit. If and when that occurred, I would receive a percentage of those profits. It's called a back-ended deal in the business. Sometimes it works out, sometimes it doesn't.

The amount of money paid me upon signing

was irrelevant, however. I was much more concerned that *Knock 'Em Dead* would actually be the basis for a Broadway play. My enthusiasm was heightened by certain things Matt had insisted be in the agreement. I was to be consulted about all aspects of the production, including the adaptation, casting, staging, and marketing. But there was a clause giving the playwright, Aaron Manley, and the director, still to be named, final say. I wasn't dismayed about that. After all, I was a neophyte when it came to theater and was pleased simply to be in a position to make suggestions.

The schedule, according to Matt, was for the play to open in March, six months from now. Such a delay didn't faze me; I was used to extended waits between turning in a book and seeing it in the bookstores.

I received a call from Aaron Manley three weeks after returning to Maine.

"How are you?" I asked.

"Quite well. You?"

"Fine. I'm working on the plot for my next novel."

"Any chance of putting it aside and coming to New York? I'm ready to start talking about our script."

"Well, yes, of course."

"Next week? Schrumm's office will send tickets."

"That will be fine."

We agreed upon a date and ended the conversation.

That night, I had dinner with members of the symphony orchestra's board of directors in a private room at a new restaurant that had opened a few months earlier, Tedeschi's Grill. Peter Eder, our conductor and musical director, gave an amusing retrospective of the first concert season. It was over dessert that talk shifted to *Knock 'Em Dead* being headed for Broadway.

"If they need a musical director," Eder said, "I'm available."

"A musical murder mystery," said a board member, laughing. "That would be a first."

"No, it wouldn't," Eder countered. "Turning grim subjects into musicals is all the rage these days."

"April Larsen is playing the lead?" someone else said.

"The last I heard. I'm going to New York next week to begin working with the playwright who'll be adapting the book."

"Who's that?"

"Aaron Manley."

Blank stares all around.

"Of course, we'll all be invited to opening night," Tim Purdy said. Tim was treasurer of the chamber of commerce and a member of the orchestra's board.

"Of course," I said, "assuming there *is* an opening night."

"Why do you say that, Jess?"

"These things don't always get off the ground. At least that's what my agent tells me."

Tim drove me home after the dinner.

"Is it really possible that the play won't be produced?" he asked.

"I'm confident it will, but I want to be a realist. I've had books optioned to Hollywood studios that never made it to the screen."

"But this will be different," he said. "You'll be the toast of the Great White Way."

"I hope you're right, Tim. Thanks for the lift. It was a great first season for the orchestra."

The following Tuesday I flew from Bangor to New York and met with Aaron Manley and Harry Schrumm at Schrumm's offices above a Chinese restaurant on West Fifty-first Street, next door to the Mark Hellinger Theater. Besides Schrumm and Manley, there were a man and woman who were introduced as being from Scott Associates, a Broadway publicity firm that would handle the marketing of *Knock 'Em Dead*, and the director Schrumm had chosen, an older British gentleman named Cyrus Walpole.

Schrumm led the meeting.

"Aaron has come up with a very rough first draft of the show," he said. "It's good, needs refining, but it'll work. Maybe you'll have some ideas once you read it, Jessica."

"That certainly was fast," I said.

"I suggest you get together after this meeting and start working," Schrumm said. "How long are you in town?"

"Three days."

"Good. That'll give you time to huddle with Linda, too."

"Who's Linda?" I asked.

"Linda Amsted. She'll be casting the show. She's already gone through her files and come up with possibilities for the husband, the two sons, the daughter, the detective—how many characters are there?"

"Eight," Walpole said. He was a corpulent man who carried it well. His beard was white and neatly cropped, his complexion above the beard line ruddy. He was one of those people I take an instant liking to, a gentle man who laughed easily and who didn't seem consumed with a need to inject himself into the conversation. Of course, I knew nothing about his professional credentials but assumed I'd be given them in due time. "One of them is marginal, I think," Walpole said. "The younger son's lady friend." His British accent was charming. "How do you feel about her, Mrs. Fletcher?"

"I thought she was important to the story," I said, "in that she ends up acting as the younger son's conscience in a sense."

"Yes, good point, I'd say, although Samantha functions in rather the same capacity. By eliminating the younger woman, we have a tantalizing sexual tension that could develop between mother and son."

"I didn't have that in mind," I said.

Schrumm waved his ring-laden hand and said, "Look, this can all be worked out. Jessica, I want you to confer with Aaron for the next couple of days. I'll set up a meeting with Linda Amsted for you to go over the photos and bios she's pulled. I'll need you back in New York three weeks from now for the backers' audition."

"I'm sorry, but I don't understand."

"Aaron will have fleshed out some scenes by then, and Linda will cast for the reading. I've got Jill and Arnie Factor salivating at the thought of backing *Knock 'Em Dead*. You met them at Windows on the World."

"Yes." I didn't mention their less-than-complimentary comments about him.

"They're starstruck and filthy rich, love rubbing elbows with famous people. I'll arrange a quiet dinner with them when you're here."

"They said they'd like to get together when I'm in town."

"Which brings up a good point," Priscilla Hoye, one of the publicists, said. "We'll be treading heavily on your name value, Mrs. Fletcher, when we actually start hyping the show. We should get plenty of TV time offering you up as a guest."

Schrumm stood and ended the meeting. "Check in with me before you head home, Jessica. I'll have a firm date for the backers' audition by then."

A group of us left his office and stood on the street.

"Might I suggest we retreat to dinner and continue this fruitful discussion?" Walpole said. Priscilla Hoye and her partner in Scott Associates, Joseph Scott, demurred: "We have nothing to offer until you're further down the road," he said. "Nice meeting you, Mrs. Fletcher. Sounds like it's going to be a winner."

The next three days were intense and exhausting. Cyrus Walpole joined Aaron and me in our working sessions and had many good suggestions to offer, as did Aaron. I felt very much a third wheel, but kept reminding myself that I'd entered into a strange and alien world with which I had no experience. Still, I held my ground when a suggestion was made with which I disagreed, and both men were quick to acknowledge my ideas and consider them. But I had no illusions.

As the contract clearly stated, they were the ones with the final say on all creative matters. All I could hope for was a fair hearing of my concerns and ideas, and a willingness to honor the fact that the play would be based upon what I'd created—every character, every twist of plot, every nuance of the relationship between members of my fictitious family.

The three days in New York passed quickly, and I flew home knowing I'd soon be returning for the backers' audition. I loved every minute of working with theater professionals whose goal was to produce the best possible stage drama from my book.

I also realized this was going to be a lot more time consuming than I'd bargained for.

What price fame?

As it turned out, a lot.

Chapter 5

The backers' audition was delayed, but that didn't mean I wasn't back in Manhattan as scheduled. Instead of attending a reading at which potential backers of *Knock 'Em Dead* decided whether to invest, I sat with casting director Linda Amsted in a darkened, inactive theater on West Forty-ninth Street for an open casting call to which hundreds of actors and actresses flocked, each hoping to become one of the characters I'd created.

There was something exhilarating, yet sad, about the process; all that talent vying for work but only a few standing a realistic chance of succeeding.

Linda Amsted's reputation as a casting director for Broadway shows and Hollywood films was exalted. I understood why after having spent two hours with her in her offices during my previous visit to New York. She had thousands of actors and actresses on her computers, their photos just a click of the mouse away, their voices stored for instant retrieval through speakers wired into the computers. I agreed with every one of her choices of actors and actresses to play the characters I'd created in *Knock 'Em Dead*. Of course, April Larsen had already been cast as Samantha, the lead in the story. But she hadn't come through Linda Amsted. She'd been handpicked by Harry Schrumm, a decision with which I wholeheartedly agreed.

After the first dozen had read from random pages of script written by Aaron Manley—he arrived an hour later, accompanied by the director, Cyrus Walpole—I leaned over to Linda and asked, "How many people will be auditioning?"

She laughed. "You never know with an open call, Jessica. Could be thousands."

"There are that many actors and actresses looking for work in New York?"

"Tens of thousands," she said. "A lot of them don't have the talent to legitimately call themselves actors or actresses, but their dreams keep them going." She lowered her voice. "I already know who I want, the ones I showed you in my office. But holding an open audition satisfies the unions."

That struck me as cruel.

"Of course," she continued, "you never know

when the next Pacino or Hoffman or Jim Carrey will show up and change everything."

"How often does that happen?"

"About once every ten years. But it isn't a wasted exercise for them. I cast a lot of plays and films. They're in my computer along with my notes about how they perform at this audition. Next!"

The actors and actresses Linda had chosen from her files to play the roles in the play—the father, two sons, daughter, younger son's girlfriend, and the detective—showed up at various times during the day and read as though they'd just walked in off the street. I assumed that was for show. No matter. I watched them with special interest since they ostensibly would bring my characters to life on the stage. I was impressed. Although they stood on a bare stage and read from a script, they immediately assumed the characters they were playing, *becoming* those people.

The actor who would play the father was, according to the bio on the back of his eight-by-ten black-and-white glossy photo, a veteran character actor of many plays and movies. I hadn't known his name—Joseph McCartney—but he was one of those I-know-the-face-but-I-can't-put-a-name-to-it performers. He was sixty-two years old, quite bald but with salt-and-pepper hair at the temples, and had a commanding baritone voice.

The two actors Linda had chosen to play the sons were different physically, so much so that I asked her whether it would make it difficult for the audience to accept that they were from the same family.

"I like the contrast," she said. "I discussed it with Cy and Aaron and they agree there's something positive in having different physical types. Not that unusual. You see it all the time, siblings looking nothing like each other. Besides, it's the way you wrote the characters."

She was right. I'd written the sons as opposites, the older son, Jerry, a brooding, physically imposing character who tended to solve problems with force rather than finesse; the younger son, Joshua, frail, pale, and sensitive, an introvert who loved books as much as his brother enjoyed pumping up his muscles on gym equipment in his room.

"Isn't he wonderful?" Linda said as the actor playing Jerry read. "There's a brute force quality to him, a young Brando-like sensuality."

"Yes, I see that," I said. He had a square, rugged face framed by a helmet of black curls. He wore tight jeans and a black T-shirt that showed off his impressive physique. His name was Brett Burton.

Linda's choice of actor to play Josh, the younger brother, was David Potts, not an especially theatrical name and probably the one with which he was born. He had almost a mystical quality about him, a dreamer, ethereal and introspective. I thought of Montgomery Clift and James Dean. He read a particularly wrenching scene between him and the father that brought tears to my eyes.

The daughter, eighteen years old and named Waldine, "Wally" (I have a close friend, Waldine Peckham, and named the character after her) was bubbly and full of life, at least as I'd envisioned her when creating the role. Hanna Shawn, the actress preselected to play her, was certainly older than eighteen, although she did have a youthful quality.

"Isn't she a little old to play Wally?" I asked.

"No," Linda replied. "Cy and Aaron have never been comfortable having the character in her teens. They want her in her midtwenties."

"Oh? No one mentioned that to me."

"I agree with them."

"But the way I wrote her, she brings a teenager's spark of life into what's become a heavy, ominous household."

"You'll have to discuss that with Cy and Aaron."

With that, the director and playwright arrived and slipped into seats next to us. It occurred to me that the reason they hadn't bothered showing up earlier was because the talent for the show had been preordained.

"What do you think?" Walpole asked in a whisper as Ms. Shawn read from the script.

"It's an impressive array of talent," I whispered back. "When did you decide to make Wally older?"

"When Harry told us to."

"Harry? Harry Schrumm?"

"Yes, quite. It's called rewriting the character to fit the talent."

"I don't understand."

"Harry wants Hanna Shawn in the show."

"Even if she isn't right for the part?"

His chuckle was muffled. "I don't mean to be crass, Jessica, but she's part of Harry's stable."

"Stable? A girlfriend?"

"A genteel way of putting it."

"I see." The proverbial casting couch at work? Obviously Broadway, like Hollywood, was no place for the naive.

There were two other roles to fill. They, too, had been determined earlier by Linda Amsted in concert with Walpole and Manley.

The younger brother's girlfriend, Marcia, was to be played by an intense young actress, Jenny Forrest. As I watched her audition—or go through the motions of auditioning—I realized she was perfect for the part. The character I'd created was as introverted as Joshua, a perfect match. She'd dressed appropriately for the audition, a loose, simple, black dress that reached her ankles, hair pulled back into a severe chignon, no makeup, and wearing large, round glasses. Marcia was, as I saw her, a mousy, unpopular young woman who never turned a male head until meeting Josh, and who saw him as her salvation, her proverbial knight in shining armor, a sensitive boy who matched her insecurity and who saw beyond her looks into a good and decent soul.

"She's wonderful," I said to Aaron Manley. "Is she that way in person?"

"No. In real life she's a conniving, ambitious young woman who skirts with being vicious."

"Really? Then she's quite an actress."

"Yeah."

He fell silent as Linda thanked Ms. Forrest for coming, told her she'd be called back if she made the cut, and announced a break for lunch. It was three o'clock. "We'll take an hour and then audition for the detective," she announced.

Sandwiches were brought in from a local deli. As we ate, some of the auditioning talent tried to engage Linda in conversation, but she coolly, professionally avoided them. Holding their fates in her hands was a formidable position of power, and I understood her reluctance to get close to those vying for her attention and approval. Still, their enthusiasm and charm were infectious; I wanted to cast every one of them.

"Is Harry coming by?" Manley asked between bites of an overstuffed pastrami sandwich.

"Not if we're lucky," Walpole said, laughing to mitigate the comment's negative overtones.

"I still have trouble with Burton playing the older brother," Manley said.

"Why?" I asked.

"I don't like him. No, to be more accurate, I don't like his type."

"The perfect 'type' to play Jerry," Amsted said matter-of-factly.

"And Harry agrees with you, of course," Manley said, unable to disguise the anger in his voice.

"Why shouldn't he?" she replied. "He trusts my judgment."

"Linda has Harry's undivided attention," Cy Walpole said coyly.

"The hell she does," Manley said. "Just one of many."

"I resent that," Amsted said.

"Resent it all you want, Linda. What have you got, a thing going with Burton, too? He *is* a hunk, but he's a little young for you, isn't he?"

She stood, dropped her half-eaten sandwich on the table, and walked away.

"Took your nasty pills this morning, I see," Walpole said.

"Sensitive, are we?" Manley said. "Linda has *your* undivided attention, too?"

Walpole rolled his eyes, stood, and shook his head. "Working in the theater would be a joy if one didn't have to put up with writers." He looked at me and said, "Present company excluded, of course."

"That's what's nice about writing novels," I said. "Just me and my word processor. Excuse me."

I followed in Linda's direction and found her smoking a cigarette and sitting on stairs leading up to the theater's balcony.

"Pompous ass," she muttered.

"I assume you're referring to Aaron."

"Jerk. I can't believe Harry brought him on board to write the script."

"From what I've read, he's done a good job. I'm surprised how faithfully he's adhered to the book." I sat beside her.

She guffawed. "That's for now, Jessica, for the auditions and the backers' dog-and-pony show. Once the show is cast and the money is in Harry's pocket, Manley will start changing every word. You'll be lucky to recognize what you wrote."

I thought for a moment before saying, "It's in the contract that I'm to be consulted on the script."

Another guffaw. " 'Consulted.' But Aaron has final say. Believe what I tell you. He's a snake, crawls on his belly, especially where Harry's concerned.''

I made an instant decision not to become involved any further in whatever problems existed among them. All I hoped was that their personal squabbles and professional jealousies wouldn't get in the way of turning *Knock 'Em Dead* into a Broadway play of which I could be proud.

At the same time, my natural curiosity kicked into gear. As a writer, I have a natural interest in people and what makes them tick, their professional lives and how they balance it with their personal ones, especially the interaction, personal and professional, between them. That inquiring tendency of mine has led me into trouble in the past, including finding myself smack dab in the middle of *real* murder. But hard as I try, I'm unable to turn it off, often to Seth Hazlitt's chagrin.

Was Linda Amsted romantically involved with Harry Schrumm, and/or with the virile actor Brett Burton? Had the actress Hanna Shawn been cast as the daughter, Waldine, because she was part of Schrumm's "stable"? It looked like the mounting of *Knock 'Em Dead* had the makings of a novel of its own.

Manley and Walpole left right after lunch. I wasn't privy to the conversation between them while I sat with Linda Amsted, but judging from the looks on their faces, it hadn't been pleasant.

Even the perpetually jovial Cyrus Walpole scowled and didn't say good-bye as he departed the theater.

Two weeks later, I returned to Manhattan for the backers' audition, which was held in the evening at Harry Schrumm's spacious, somewhat dismal apartment on Manhattan's West Side. There was a masculine casualness to it, and it was every bit the bachelor pad. Schrumm had been married four times.

"Welcome, Jessica," Schrumm said, greeting me at the door, wearing a blood-red silk smoking jacket. "You're the final arrival."

"Am I late?"

"No, but the others have been here for hours. At least it seems that way when you're dealing with creative types. Come in, come in. Champagne?"

It was obvious the Factors were the guests of honor the moment I entered the apartment. They were formally dressed again (did they sleep in formal clothing?), and were seated in matching high-back wing chairs directly in front of what would be the stage. One end of the expansive living room had been cleared of furniture, except for red director's chairs with white frames lined up facing the wing chairs. The apartment's lights had been lowered; four spotlights mounted on flimsy stands were aimed at the makeshift stage.

Casting director Linda Amsted was there along with the entire cast. A young blonde woman—I judged her to be in her early twenties—hung on Schrumm's arm. She wore extremely tight black slacks and a teal blouse unbuttoned almost to her stomach, exposing a large amount of bosom. I would learn later her name was Pamela South and that she was an actress. Another member of Harry Schrumm's stable?

A party atmosphere prevailed. Drinks flowed freely, and conversations were spirited. Most of the cast members sought me out and we discussed how I saw their characters in the play—what their *motivations* were for doing and saying certain things. They were a pleasant group of people, perhaps with the exception of Aaron Manley and the actor playing Jerry, the older brother, who sustained the brooding disposition he'd displayed during auditions.

I was in the midst of a conversation with April Larsen when Schrumm stepped to the center of the room, asked for quiet, and announced, "It's time for the show to go on." He nodded to Jill and Arnie Factor in the wing chairs, turned, and said, "For those of you who've never attended a backers' audition, let me just say that the purpose is to convince wonderful patrons of the arts like

Mr. and Mrs. Factor to choose this particular show in which to pour their money." The Factors laughed. "As we all know, competition has recently heated up on Broadway. It's in its renaissance, thanks in part to our crime-fighting mayor and the deep pockets of Disney. That means investors like our esteemed guests this evening have more shows from which to choose. But I know that in *Knock 'Em Dead*, written by one of the world's preeminent writers of murder mysteries, Jessica Fletcher, we have something to give them that will not only render next season's offerings anemic in comparison, it will run on the Great White Way for years to come." He cast a sly glance at the Factors. "Which, of course, means generating a handsome return for these dear people for years to come, too."

"Another *Mousetrap*," Cy Walpole said, exuberantly.

"Here, here!" someone shouted.

"Then let us raise the curtain on Broadway's next major theatrical triumph, *Knock 'Em Dead*."

The next hour went smoothly. The actors and actresses performed selected scenes Aaron Manley had written. He'd chosen the most dramatic ones from the script we'd worked on together, but deliberately left out the most dramatic of all, the final scene when the detective confronts the family and identifies the killer. The actor playing the detective

was a tall, angular, handsome fellow, Charles
Flowers, who spoke with a trace of a Southern
accent, and who captured perfectly, I felt, the character in the book. They all did, for that matter,
especially April Larsen, whose portrayal of the
mother was, in my estimation, brilliant. The director provided amusing, clarifying bridges between
the unconnected scenes.

"Bravo!" Schrumm shouted when the performance was finished and he'd turned up lights in
the apartment.

"No fair," Arnie Factor said, standing. "Who
dunnit?"

"You'll have to pay for that," Schrumm replied,
good-naturedly.

"We'll have to read the book," Factor said.

"That would be cheating," Schrumm said. "Besides, we might just change the ending."

Eyes shifted to me.

"You wouldn't allow them to do that, would
you, Mrs. Fletcher?" Jill Factor said.

"Over my dead body."

"Spoken like a true crime writer," said Joe
McCartney, who played the father.

Two uniformed women emerged from the
kitchen and placed platters of food on the dining
room table, and drinks again were served.

"How long will it take for them to decide
whether to invest?" I whispered to Linda Amsted.

"Oh, they'll invest," she said. "They loved every second of it. They'll negotiate with Harry, try to up their take and insist on keeping costs down, but they'll put their money on the table, or in this case in Harry's pocket. You can take that to the bank."

"What's next?" I asked Schrumm as everyone prepared to leave.

"Nothing involving you, Jessica. Aaron will settle in and do the real adaptation and—"

" '*Real*?' This wasn't *real*?"

"You know what I mean. A finished script. These were just scenes to entice the Factors into backing the show."

"Yes, I knew that," I said, "but I hope he continues being true to the book."

"Oh, he will, Jessica, my dear. Don't worry about that. You go on back to that quaint little town of yours in Maine, enjoy the holidays, and get ready to return next February when rehearsals go into full swing."

"I assume I'll be conferring with Aaron as he progresses on the script."

"Of course. Work that out with him, only don't expect too close a collaboration, at least not while he's churning out the final draft. Better to leave him alone. He works better that way."

The Factors stopped to congratulate me on their way out. "We've invested in many of Harry's productions," Arnie said, "but this one has a scent unlike any of the others."

"Scent?"

"Sweet smell of success." He leaned close to my ear and said, "We're in, Jessica, only don't tell Harry that. I like to let him sweat for a few days. Enhances the bargaining position."

"We insist you be our guests at dinner the next time you're in town," Jill said. "At our penthouse. You'll love the views of Manhattan."

Chapter 6

Two Months Later

Time always seems to pass more quickly as you become older, but my involvement in readying *Knock 'Em Dead* for a Broadway opening really chewed up the weeks. Despite Harry Schrumm having said that there was nothing for me to do until serious rehearsals started in February, I spent what felt like half my life in New York City, a virtual commuter to New York, the Westin Central Park South Hotel my second home. Of course, not every trip south had to do with *Knock 'Em Dead*. There were meetings with my publisher and my agent regarding a new novel I'd started, and I made a few journeys to the Big Apple to visit friends and to do some Christmas shopping in Manhattan's wonderful stores.

But Schrumm, Manley, and Walpole seemed to want my input at various stages, and I was more than happy to accommodate. It made me feel like a Broadway insider, a true part of the creative team readying the play for its March opening.

As Vaughan had predicted, the Broadway serial killer's four murders had become a national story, and I kept up with it both at home and when in Manhattan. He hadn't struck since having killed the producer in September at the Von Feurston Theater. The New York PD had established a special task force headed by a detective named Henry Hayes. A reward for the capture and conviction of the killer was being offered by the New York Theater Guild. A number of theaters reported adding extra security to their staff, and one actress appearing in a Broadway musical told the reporter she dreaded going to work and would continue to feel that way until "the fiend is caught and behind bars."

I made it a point to be in Cabot Cove for Christmas, a special time of year in the lovely town I call home. Christmas Day had dawned crystal clear and surprisingly warm for that time of year, and I joined my friends in a round of afternoon get-togethers where the spirit of the season washed over us, peace on earth and good will toward men very much alive in Cabot Cove, even though it wasn't in so many other less fortunate parts of the world.

"Plan on stayin' a while?" Seth Hazlitt asked as we sipped eggnog at his house.

"Until February. I'm behind on so many things, including my newest book. Vaughan has been wonderful pushing the delivery date back, but there's a limit to how far he can let it slide. The producer wants me in New York for the final three weeks of rehearsal in February. I'll just stay there until previews start. This commuting back and forth is getting old."

"As I imagine it would be. Susan was in for a checkup yesterday. She wants to put together another theater group to coincide with *Knock 'Em Dead*'s opening."

"That would be wonderful. I've talked to Harry Schrumm about being able to bring friends to the rehearsals. He wasn't especially keen on the idea but said it would be okay. Why don't you plan to spend a week in February in New York, Seth. Bring some of the others with you. To be honest, I sometimes feel a little lonely there."

"I might be able to swing that. The patient load slows down about then. I'll see what I can do."

"That would be wonderful. Going to the concert?"

"*Ayuh*. Wouldn't miss that."

That night we gathered in the high school auditorium and listened to the orchestra conducted by Peter Eder play Christmas music, culminating with a sing-a-long led by one of our churches' musical directors, and featuring the lovely voices of a children's choir. We gathered at Richard Koser's house following the concert to sing around the piano and extend the day's good feelings. Richard was a photographer who'd taken most of my book jacket photos.

"Did Seth tell you about the theater package I'm putting together?" Susan Shevlin asked.

"Yes. It sounds wonderful. I told him it would be okay for my friends to attend some rehearsals if you're in New York the last few weeks of February. And I have twenty seats for opening night of previews. My agent had that written into the contract."

"That's wonderful. We can catch a few rehearsals and be there en masse opening night."

"For previews, not the *real* opening, Susan. There'll probably be last-minute bugs to iron out before the official opening."

"So what? We'll feel like we're special, in-the-know." She giggled. "We're all so proud of you, Jess."

I blushed, and joined in the singing of a spirited, out-of-tune version of "God Rest Ye Merry Gentlemen."

* * *

"I don't care," Cyrus Walpole bellowed from the stage of the Drummond Theater where rehearsals for *Knock 'Em Dead* were underway. "You're a vile, twisted, evil woman and I will not tolerate you for another minute."

His tirade was directed at Jenny Forrest, the actress playing Marcia, the younger brother's girlfriend in the show. I'd been sensing that a blowup was imminent; Walpole and Jenny had been at each other's throats ever since I returned to New York and started attending daily rehearsals. Jenny was a wonderful actress. Simultaneously, she was a foul-mouthed, conniving young woman who seemed always to be at the center of turmoil.

"Don't you dare speak to me that way," she shouted back at Walpole, "you fat, disgusting slob."

For a moment I thought Cy was going to physically attack her. Instead, he came to where I sat with the casting director, Linda Amsted. His face was crimson with anger, and he visibly shook. "Get her out of here, Linda, and find someone else to play Marcia."

"Just like that," Linda said, shaking her head. "She makes a marvelous Marcia, Cy. You're the director. Figure out how to direct her."

"Don't lay the responsibility on me for taming that horrible woman," Walpole said. "You chose her for the part. You fire her and bring in someone I can work with."

"Firing is Harry's job," she said. "He's the producer."

"I've already spoken with Harry about it. He says you're to handle these things."

As they snarled at each other, the rest of the cast, and some of the crew, watched from the stage with bemused interest. Jenny Forrest lit a small cigar and perched on a tall stool, a crooked smile on her round, plain face.

"Excuse us," Linda said to me, standing and leading Walpole to the lobby where they could continue their conversation in less public surroundings.

April Larsen left the stage and sat next to me. "This is extremely distressing," she said.

"It certainly is," I said.

"Frankly, I think our esteemed casting director has done a frightful job of choosing a cast."

"Oh? I thought—"

"The chemistry between actor and actress on stage is crucial to a play's success, Jessica. When Harry asked me to play the mother—no, begged me is more apt—he assured me he would surround me with New York's best talent. He certainly has gone back on his word." She forced a laugh. "But that isn't unusual for Harry. He's the biggest liar I've ever known. You should speak up, Jessica. After all, your name is up there on the marquee along with mine. It's *your* story that's being presented to the public. It's *your* reputation at stake."

I started to respond but she burst into tears, stood, and disappeared into the shadows.

I sat alone and pondered what had just occurred. Although I was not experienced in theater, certainly not at the Broadway level, it struck me as unusual that a show's casting director would be so intimately involved in every aspect of the production. My assumption was that once a cast had been chosen, and it had been approved by the producer, director, and lord knows who else, the casting director's job would be done and she'd move on to casting the next play or movie.

But it seemed that Linda Amsted wore many hats for *Knock 'Em Dead*, including being a den mother to the actors and actresses she'd chosen. April Larsen's unkind comments about her didn't set well with me. Of everyone involved in the production, Linda was my favorite, and we'd forged a friendship. I liked her personally and respected her professionally. The rumors that she was having an affair with Harry Schrumm, and perhaps with the brooding actor, Brett Burton, were just that to me, rumors. Even if true, it was her business. I could see how men would be attracted to her. She wasn't beautiful by any standard, but she exuded a quiet sensuality, lips full, dark eyes testifying to having lived a bit, a full but trim figure she maintained by exercising regularly at a gym near her office.

Without Walpole to direct the rehearsal, the cast dispersed. Lunch was scheduled for one, but since it was now a little after noon, they left the theater for an extended break. I went to the stage where playwright Aaron Manley sat pecking away at his laptop.

"Still making changes to the script?" I asked.

"Yeah. I don't like the way the scene between the detective and the mother plays out in Act Two."

I pulled up a folding chair and read what was on his screen. I didn't like what I saw, but was reluctant to be critical, considering the frayed nerves permeating the theater that day.

"I suppose you don't like it," he said.

"I just don't think the detective would say something like that."

He sat back with force, clenched his teeth, and said, "How would you know what a detective would say?"

"How? Because I've been writing murder mysteries my entire adult life. I've created dozens of fictitious detectives and have spent plenty of time with real ones."

"Then *you* write the script." He stood, almost

knocking over his chair, and walked away. As he did, Cy Walpole emerged from the lobby with Linda Amsted.

"Where's Jenny?" Linda asked.

I shrugged, still upset about the exchange with Manley.

"She's being replaced," Walpole said. "Our Miss Jenny Forrest is a *former* member of this production."

"Isn't it late to replace her?" I asked.

"Not for our beloved casting director," Walpole said. "She made the original mistake in hiring Jenny. She can come up with her replacement."

"She was cast with your approval, Cy," Linda said.

"No," he said. "She was cast with Harry's approval, which all of us knew would happen. I've always felt that when a casting director is too cozy with the producer, such mistakes are bound to happen."

Linda's eyes narrowed, and her lip trembled.

"We called Harry," Walpole said. "He's on his way. Linda has his permission to throw that insufferable woman out of this theater and out of my life."

"Why does Linda have to do it?" I asked. "Why doesn't Harry fire her? He's the producer."

Walpole's smile and voice were annoyingly condescending. He patted me on the shoulder and said, "It's not your concern, dear Jessica. And don't worry. Linda will find a new and better actress to play Marcia. Everything will be just fine. Trust me."

I went to the lobby and called Matt Miller to see if he was free for lunch. He wasn't. Neither was Vaughan Buckley. I opted to not try other friends in New York and set out in search of a quiet spot for a solo lunch. I'd no sooner stepped from the theater on to West Forty-fourth Street when Jill and Arnold Factor got out of a cab and stopped me. "We were hoping you'd still be here," Arnie said. "Free for lunch?"

"As a matter of fact I am."

"Good," said Jill. "Forty-four, in the Royalton, is just down the street."

As we set off, I realized that Jill wasn't as tall as she appeared to be. She was fond of shoes with spike heels, adding a good four inches to her height. I've never understood how women can wear such shoes. I tried it once and felt as though I was on stilts.

The restaurant, they told me during our short walk, was named because its address was Forty-four West Forty-fourth Street. According to them, it was one of New York's latest "in" spots, a favorite of Broadway luminaries and publishing tycoons; its unofficial name was the "Conde Nast Lunchroom." The decor was, I suppose, new age—spare and gleaming and smacking of high-tech. The Factors weren't strangers there; we were immediately led to a prime table by a gracious maître d'. Arnold ordered an expensive bottle of white wine despite my objections to anything alcoholic that early in the day and quickly got to why they were looking for me.

"What's going on with the show?" Jill asked. She was dressed in a pretty, soft, rose-colored pant suit and wore a large, taupe floppy brimmed hat of the sort usually seen on Southern belles. Her voice didn't match her outfit's mellowness. There was steel in it.

"What do you mean?" I asked.

"*Knock 'Em Dead*," Arnold said, sniffing and tasting the wine, proclaiming it satisfactory, and leaning closer to me. "We understand there are major problems."

"Oh, you mean the conflict over Ms. Forrest. She was fired this morning. Linda Amsted is looking for a replacement."

"We know about that," Jill said. "We just came from Harry's office. We're talking about money."

"Money? I'm sorry, I don't understand."

"No, I suppose you don't," Arnold said. He looked at his wife as though seeking permission to continue. She narrowed her eyes and nodded. He said, "Tell me about these new people Harry has added to the production staff."

"What new people?"

He pulled a slip of paper from his blazer pocket and consulted it. "Walter Schrumm, production coordinator. Nancy Schrumm, marketing coordinator. Marlena Mikowski, liaison to the mayor's office of cultural affairs."

Jill added as an aside, "Evidently, Ms. Mikowski is related to Harry by marriage."

"I'm afraid I don't understand," I said. "I haven't heard of these people, and I've been at rehearsals every day."

"Exactly," Arnold said, bitterness in his voice. "Another Harry Schrumm scam. It's called adding ghost employees to the payroll to make sure there aren't any profits."

I started to say something, but Jill cut me off. "Harry did less of it with the last few shows we invested in, and we could live with it. But now it looks like he's back to his old tricks, eating up any profits before the show even opens."

"He's padded the payroll?"

Jill's laugh was scornful. "Oh, yes. Oldest trick in the book. Routine in Hollywood, and becoming so on Broadway."

"I obviously have a lot to learn," I said as a waiter came for our lunch order. "As far as I'm concerned, I've written a book that's being turned into a play, hopefully a good and successful one.

The business side of it interests me, of course, but isn't my primary concern."

"It should be," Arnold said, ordering three warm chicken salads without bothering to ask my preference. "Your contract calls for you to get a piece of the action."

"A percentage of the profits," I said. "That's right."

"There won't be any profits if Harry has his way," Jill said, "no matter how successful the show is."

"Then why would you invest in something with him?" I asked.

"Because this play can be a Broadway block-buster, Jessica, with a long and profitable run. We didn't put up a million six without being convinced of that."

I suppose my wide eyes testified that I was surprised the Factors had invested that much money in *Knock 'Em Dead*. Arnold said, "Putting on a Broadway show isn't cheap. Musicals can cost five times that. That's why we avoid them. We backed your show because of you and your reputation. This play has all the trappings of success, big time, but not if Harry's allowed to spend money without any checks and balances."

"I certainly agree with accountability where large sums of money are involved. But why are you telling *me* this? If I feel I'm being cheated, I'm sure my agent and lawyer will step in."

"By then it will be too late," Jill said. "Look, the three of us have something major at stake here. We're too busy to hang around the theater for rehearsals. But you're there. We want you to be our eyes and ears, let us know what's going on."

I sat back and chewed my cheek before replying: "I'd be uncomfortable in that role."

"Why?" Arnold asked.

"I have natural curiosity as a writer, but that doesn't extend to being an official snoop."

"Even when your financial future is at stake?" Arnold asked, smiling smugly.

"Even then. I'll discuss this with my agent. I appreciate your concerns as the people who've put up so much money for the show, but I'm afraid you'll have to get your information from other sources."

"Jessica is right," Jill said, injecting sweetness into her voice. "Let's eat. The salad looks wonderful."

We parted in front of the hotel.

"We were wrong in trying to use you as a conduit of information," Arnold said. "Please accept our apologies."

"None needed. Thank you for a lovely lunch. The salad was wonderful."

I slowly walked back to the theater, stopping to window shop on my way. I was only twenty feet from the theater entrance when the doors opened and Linda Amsted emerged, followed closely by Jenny Forrest. The actress carried a knife. "You rotten bitch!" Jenny screamed, holding the knife above her head and closing the gap between them.

Linda backed toward the curb, hands held in a defensive position. "Don't be stupid, Jenny," she said. "Don't make a bad situation worse. We can work this out."

Dozens of people stopped and watched the confrontation. I moved quickly, placing myself between the actress and the casting director. "Jenny!" I said in my most authoritative voice. "Put that knife down!"

She became immobile, the knife still raised over her head. She then smiled and said, "Spoken by the famous mystery writer, Jessica Fletcher. Maybe I should cut *your* heart out."

"What I suggest is that you drop the knife, come back inside the theater, and talk this out. Maybe if you—"

She moved so quickly I didn't have a chance to respond. In an instant, she bolted at me and brought the knife down with force against my chest. A bright light flashed. People gasped. A few women screamed, including Linda Amsted.

I don't know what I did, or said. The shock was

too great. All I know is that Jenny started laughing as the knife, its blade having retracted into the handle, fell to her feet. My hand went involuntarily to my chest. No blood, just an ache from the stage prop having been shoved so hard against me.

"You'll hear from me again," Jenny said, still laughing as she slowly pushed her way through the gathered crowd, disappearing behind them.

"Are you all right?" Linda asked, coming to me and picking up the knife.

"Yes, I think so. That young woman is seriously demented."

"Tell me about it. When I told her she was through, she went berserk. Sorry it ended with you taking the blow."

"I've taken worse," I said. "But I think I'd better go inside and sit down. I'm suddenly feeling a little tired."

Chapter 7

I sat with Linda Amsted in the theater for a half hour until I'd regained my composure.

"Sure you're okay?" she asked.

"Yes, I'm fine, but I think I'll go back to the hotel."

"I'll go with you."

"No need, but thanks. I'll probably not show up for rehearsals tomorrow. I'm due for a quiet day to myself, maybe a little shopping, dive into a good book."

"Sounds like just the medicine," she said, walking me to the lobby. "Give a call if you need anything, day or night. I mean that, Jessica."

"You're very sweet, Linda. I'll stay in touch."

I took a nap that afternoon, enjoyed a quiet dinner at a small Japanese restaurant a block from the hotel, returned to my room overlooking Manhattan, changed into pajamas and robe, and read until eleven when my eyes started closing. I'd been relatively successful in blotting out the memory of the scene in front of the theater with Jenny Forrest, but once I'd fluffed up the pillows on the king-sized bed and settled in for what hopefully would be a solid night's sleep, visions of the crazed young woman lunging at me with the knife filled my brain. Although it had only been a stage prop with a retractable blade, I had no way of knowing that before the fact. In the split second it took for her to make contact, I was convinced I was about to be stabbed to death. Thinking of it made me shudder, and I pulled the covers up tight around my neck, willing myself to sleep.

I didn't dream about the incident. At least I didn't remember any such dreams when I awoke the next morning at six-thirty to the ringing phone next to the bed.

"Hello?" I said, my voice sounding as though I'd just been awakened from a deep sleep, which was the case.

"Mrs. Fletcher, this is Martin Willig, assistant manager of the hotel."

I sat up and rubbed my eyes. "Yes?"

"Terribly sorry to wake you so early, but I thought it was better for me to do it than to put the calls through."

"I'm usually up at this hour anyway. What calls?"

"The press. There are a half-dozen reporters in the lobby wanting to talk to you, including a TV crew. Journalists have been calling, too, but I instructed our telephone staff to hold those calls until I had a chance to speak with you."

"I appreciate that. Why do they want to see *me*?"

"I suppose it's because of what happened outside the theater yesterday."

"You know about that?"

He laughed. "Me and all of New York. The photo of you being attacked makes quite a front page on the *Post* this morning."

"Picture? On the *Post*?" I suddenly remembered a flash of light when Jenny attacked me. A press photographer? "Mr. Willig, could you arrange to send up the paper, along with some strong coffee, orange juice, and a croissant?"

"Of course. Ten minutes."

I'd brushed my teeth and washed my face by the time room service arrived, accompanied by Mr. Willig. He handed me the newspaper. The photo of me being "stabbed" was huge, taking up almost the entire front page. The headline read: KNOCK 'EM DEAD—FICTION OR FACT?

"Oh, my," I said.

"What a horrible thing to go through," Willig said. "Have you reported it to the police?"

"No."

"You should."

"It was just—it turned out to be a stage prop, one of those knives whose blade retracts into its handle. It couldn't have hurt me."

"Still—"

"I'll think about it. You say the press is in the lobby. Who's been calling?"

He handed me a slew of message slips, which I quickly perused. The calls were from media, with the exception of two from Cabot Cove, one from Seth Hazlitt, the other from our sheriff, Morton Metzger.

"I appreciate the way you've handled this, Mr. Willig. Please continue to hold the calls."

"Of course. We'll put nothing through to the room. You can ring down for any new messages."

"Wonderful."

He gave me a card with his private direct extension and left.

I showered and dressed, downed the orange juice and a few sips of coffee, and called the hotel's message center. There were ten additional calls, most from the press, others from my agent, my publisher, Harry Schrumm, and the publicist, Priscilla Hoye. I returned Seth's call first.

"You all right, Jessica?" he asked the moment we were connected.

"Yes, of course."

"Why did that woman attack you yesterday?"

"How do you know about it?"

"TV, one of the morning shows ran a picture of it from some newspaper."

"It was just a silly misunderstanding, Seth. It wasn't a real knife."

"One of those publicity setups, a photo op?"

"No, it wasn't planned but—"

"Then why would somebody do somethin' like that?"

"Because—she was actually after someone else—I got in the way and . . . well, it doesn't matter. It's over. No harm done."

"Maybe you'd better head on home, Jessica. Sounds to me like crime in New York isn't down as much as that hotshot mayor says it is."

"Everything's fine, Seth. It was all just a silly mistake."

"Talk to Mort this morning?"

"No, but he left a message. I'll get back to him after I get off with you."

"Well, stay there if you will, but my advice is still for you to head back here. Having a run of unusually mild weather. Jed Richardson pulled in some nice fish down at Junction Pool yesterday."

"That sounds wonderful, but I'll have to postpone any fishing until after the show opens. It's less than two weeks until previews. Are you still coming with Susan and the others?"

"*Ayuh*, unless I'm needed there sooner."

"Why would you be—? Great. Looking forward to seeing everyone again."

Mort Metzger, too, had seen the morning TV show on which the photo from the *Post* had been displayed.

"What in God's name is going on down there, Mrs. F?" he asked.

"Just a mistake, Mort. A—a photo op. For publicity."

"That's not what the fella on TV said."

"Oh? What did he say?"

"He said the woman who attacked you was an actress in *Knock 'Em Dead* who'd been fired and was getting even."

"That's ridiculous. It wasn't even a real knife."

"Looked real enough to me in the picture. I'm sending Wendell down to New York."

"Wendell? Who's Wendell?"

"Wendell Watson, Gloria's boy. Just got himself his security guard license."

"Good for him. But why are you sending him here?"

"Keep an eye on you. Be your bodyguard. I'd come myself but can't get the time off till I come down with Susan's theater group. Wendell will fill in for me till then."

I couldn't help but laugh. "Bodyguard? I don't need a bodyguard."

"I'll be the judge of that, Jessica. You're a celebrity. Celebrities have bodyguards. There's plenty of nuts running around stalking people like you, and I have the responsibility of protecting this town's citizens, no matter where they might be."

There was nothing to be gained from arguing with him. Once Mort decided on something, there was no dissuading him.

"Where will Wendell stay while he's in New York?" I asked.

"With Gloria's brother. He lives somewhere in Brooklyn. But Wendell will be at your side every waking hour."

"That's comforting to know. I have to return some other calls. See you next week."

I was about to call Matt Miller when someone knocked at the door.

"Hello?"

"Mrs. Fletcher. It's Priscilla Hoye, from Scott Associates."

It took me a second to recognize the name. Priscilla was the publicist. I opened the door to the extent the security chain allowed.

"Hi," she said.

"Hi."

I heard voices from beyond her. "Is someone with you?" I asked.

"Press. They followed me up. Can I come in? We have to talk."

"Yes, *you* can come in. Not them."

"Of course not."

Her message was clear, to the point, and somewhat dismaying. She was thrilled with the photo on the *Post*'s front page and wanted to capitalize on it by arranging a press conference for that afternoon.

"I'd rather not do that," I said.

"You have to," she said. "This could ensure a rush to the box office. We'll play up every angle of it, including the ghost slant."

"What ghost slant?"

"Didn't you read the article in the *Post*?"

"No. I never got past my picture on the front page."

"Read it." She handed me a copy of the paper she'd brought with her.

It was a long piece on page four, bylined Martin Hollander, that pretty much captured the way it had happened. The photo was taken, Hollander wrote, by a passerby, who sold it to the *Post*.

Once the article got past the nitty-gritty, it briefly chronicled the history of the theater in which *Knock 'Em Dead* would be opening, the Drummond Theater, named after a Broadway actor of years past, Marcus Drummond. According to Hollander, Drummond had been found murdered in the theater. It carried a different name at that time, but new owners decided to rename it after the flamboyant thespian. Ever since his death, people claimed his ghost haunted the theater, appearing late at night bathed in a single spotlight that would suddenly come on, his face chalk white, lips a vivid red, a wicked cackle coming from him just before he would disappear as quickly as he'd arrived.

"I don't believe in ghosts," I said, handing the paper back to Priscilla.

She laughed. "I don't either—usually. But it's an interesting story we can play up. Here's a murder mystery about to open in a haunted theater where its namesake was murdered. An angry actress attacks America's most beloved writer of murder mysteries with a stage prop knife on the street, in front of hundreds of onlookers. And don't forget, the Broadway serial killer is still on the loose. Everything's falling into place. Please, Jessica, just one press conference. That'll take care of the media in a single shot. It's too good an opportunity to let slip."

"I suppose you're right, Priscilla, but I hadn't planned on a press conference."

"Nothing to it. I'll set it up. All you have to do is show up and answer their questions."

"What do I say about Ms. Forrest?"

"The truth. She was angry at being replaced in the show."

"I wouldn't want to hurt her."

"Don't worry about that. I'll arrange it for four this afternoon, at the theater."

"All right."

"Have I told you how terrific I think you are?"

"No, and I'd prefer that you not. All I care is that the show open to rave reviews, enough tickets are sold to make everyone happy, and that I can get back to Cabot Cove and some semblance of normalcy."

"Everything you want will happen, believe me. Don't talk to the press until this afternoon. No exclusives."

"Okay."

I called Harry Schrumm, who used the foulest language to describe Jenny Forrest, and then went on to level a barrage of criticism at everyone else connected with the play. I listened patiently until he was finished with his harangue, holding the phone away from my ear. His parting words were, "Maybe I ought to fire everybody. I'll see you at the theater at four."

After returning the other nonmedia calls, I dialed Mr. Willig's private number. "I'd like to leave the hotel," I told him, "but don't want to have to deal with the press. Is there another way out?"

"Absolutely. I'll come up to your suite straight-away and lead you myself."

It felt good to be away from the commotion and on my own. I wore sunglasses and a large hat with earmuffs to ensure that no one would recognize me and set out at a brisk pace, going nowhere in particular, just enjoying the walk. But I slowed down after not too many blocks as the sky turned gray and heavy, and a cold wind began whipping down Manhattan's manmade canyons. I smelled snow in the air.

I passed newsstands where the picture of my being attacked was prominently displayed on the front page of piles of that morning's *Post*. I stopped at a coffee shop for a cup of tea but abandoned the idea when the woman behind the counter saw through my dark glasses and said, "You're Jessica Fletcher. What a terrible thing that happened to you. That young woman ought to be behind bars." She bellowed to a man seated behind a cash register, "Hey, Morris, it's Jessica Fletcher." Everyone turned and stared.

"Excuse me," I said. "I forgot I have to be somewhere else."

I took refuge in a movie theater where a highly acclaimed new film was playing. I hated it. It was nothing but car chases and bloody bodies flying across the screen and steamy sex scenes that didn't have anything to do with the story, if there was one. The movie ended at three-fifteen. I was due at the Drummond at four. I stepped out of the movie theater into a light snow sent swirling by the wind, pulled my coat collar up tight about my neck, lowered my head into the wind, and headed for the press conference, which ranked low on any priority list I might have made.

I turned the corner on to Forty-fourth Street and saw through the snow the marquee on which *Knock 'Em Dead* glowed. I paused at the theater next to the Drummond, the Von Feurston, where the most recent Broadway serial killing had taken place. What perverted, subhuman person was going around not only killing people backstage, but adding a grotesque signature to the slayings? I shuddered at the thought and headed to the theater—*my* theater—next door, when someone approaching from the opposite direction bumped into me, almost knocking me over. I never had a clear look at the person, but I did see that it was a man wearing a gray overcoat with the collar turned up and a black knit cap pulled low over his forehead. He'd been walking fast and didn't break stride as he kept going, never pausing to apologize. I watched him disappear into the crowd on the street and tried to focus on what I could remember of him. I'd once taken a class in witness identification techniques. Ever since, I've gotten into the habit of taking in every possible detail of people I meet, under both pleasant and unpleasant circumstances. My final fleeting image of him was from the top of his wool cap down to his shoulders.

How rude, I thought as I turned and continued into the theater where Priscilla Hoye and Joe Scott stood in the lobby with Harry Schrumm and a group of reporters, including cameramen from local TV stations. They immediately started hurling questions at me, but Priscilla waved her hands and said, "Harry Schrumm, the producer of *Knock 'Em Dead*, has a statement to make. After that, Mrs. Fletcher will be available to answer questions."

She led us to a folding table at one end of the lobby where a microphone had been set up. As I followed, she looked down and asked, "What happened to your coat?"

"What do you mean?"

"It's torn."

I checked what she'd seen. Sure enough, there was a tear down the side almost a foot long.

"I can't imagine how this happened," I said.

Priscilla examined it more closely. "It's been cut," she said.

"Cut?"

"Yes, look."

I removed the coat and took a closer look. She

was right. It wasn't a tear. It had been neatly sliced.

"The man who almost knocked me down," I said to no one in particular.

"What?"

"Ah—nothing. I must have caught it on something. Let's get this over with."

Chapter 8

The press conference was less painful than anticipated and over sooner than I'd expected. Harry Schrumm's statement was impressive in its brevity; he spoke of how upsetting the attack on me was to him personally, called for a stepped-up police effort to capture the Broadway serial killer, and predicted that *Knock 'Em Dead* would one day be Broadway's longest running play.

Schrumm introduced me and I took questions from the press, most of them directed at the attack on me by Jenny Forrest. I tried to play down its significance, even laughed when describing how the knife proved to be only a stage prop.

"Will you press charges against Ms. Forrest?" I was asked.

"No."

"Was this staged as a publicity stunt to hype your play?"

"No."

"Are you afraid the Broadway serial killer will strike someone from the cast of *Knock 'Em Dead*?"

"I certainly hope not."

"Do you believe in ghosts, Mrs. Fletcher, specifically the ghost of Marcus Drummond, for whom this theater is named?"

I chuckled. "I haven't seen him yet and don't expect to. Thank you."

As the reporters drifted away, I looked across the lobby and saw a man I hadn't noticed during the press conference leaning against a wall in a far corner. Perhaps his nondescript appearance contributed to my not having taken note of him. He was of medium height, had sandy hair, and wore a tan raincoat; a beige figure absorbed by the beige lobby walls. He slowly crossed the lobby and stood a few feet from the table. Schrumm disappeared into the theater. "I'll be back in a minute," Priscilla said, chasing after a reporter.

"Mrs. Fletcher?" the man said.

"Yes?"

"I'm Lieutenant Henry Hayes, NYPD." He held out his badge.

"Police? You aren't here because of what happened, are you? It was just a silly mistake, as I explained to the press."

His smile was wide and warm. He extended his hand, which I took. "Not specifically," he said. "I'm heading up the Broadway serial killer task force."

"I read that you were. Any progress?"

"Afraid not. Got a minute?"

"Sure."

"Cup of coffee?"

"Tea is appealing."

"There's a coffee shop a few doors away."

I slipped into my coat and came around the table to join him.

"You've ripped your coat," he said.

I looked down. "I forgot. I can't imagine how it happened."

He lifted the hem and examined the tear.

"It's been cut."

"That's what Priscilla said. She's the publicist for the play."

"When did it happen?"

"I don't know. I wasn't aware of it until I arrived here an hour ago. Priscilla pointed it out to me."

"A clean cut. Must have been a very sharp object."

"I don't recall catching it on anything."

"A knife."

"A knife?"

"I'd say so. Has it been in anyone's possession other than yours?"

"No. I wore it from the hotel, went to a coffee shop, took in a movie, then came straight here."

He bit his lip and grunted.

"You don't think someone did it deliberately—do you?"

He shrugged.

"Someone bumped into me outside the theater."

"Really?"

"A man."

"Did he bump into you on the side where your coat is torn?"

I thought a moment and said, "Yes."

"What did he look like?"

"Oh, young, I think, but I can't be sure, wearing a gray overcoat and a black knit cap. The cap was pulled down low so I didn't see much of his face."

Hayes led me to a secluded corner of the lobby. "Let me show you something, Mrs. Fletcher."

He pulled an envelope from the small briefcase he carried, removed a paper from it, and handed it to me. It was a police artist's sketch of a man wearing a black knit cap pulled down over his forehead.

"Recognize him?"

"No."

"Doesn't bear any resemblance to the man who bumped into you outside?"

"It's impossible to tell," I said. "It could be the same person, but that's only because the cap is the same. As I told you, I didn't see his face clearly."

"But you saw it clearly enough to know it was a man, not a woman."

"I can't even claim that," I said. "I assume it was a man because of the clothing. He bumped me and was gone. It could have been a woman wearing a man's overcoat. A knit hat is unisex, I suppose."

He said nothing as he slipped the sketch back into the envelope and returned it to his briefcase.

"Is that a sketch of the Broadway serial killer?" I asked, not sure it was appropriate.

"We're not certain. A witness said he saw someone who looked like this coming out of the alley between this theater and the Von Feurston next door, right after the murder of a producer there. Probably means nothing, but we're following up every lead, no matter how insignificant."

"Of course. Mr. Hayes—Detective Hayes, is it?"

"Detective. Lieutenant. Henry."

"Why are you here today? You didn't know about my torn coat and the episode on the street until just now."

"Just following a pattern."

"What sort of pattern?"

"A pattern of where the killer has struck. We've laid out a grid, and there seems to be a design of sorts. His first two killings—and we're operating under the assumption that the killer is male—the first two killings occurred in theaters that were side by side. The third occurred four blocks from the original two. Now this one at the Von Feurston."

"Which breaks the pattern."

"Yes, unless he now intends to repeat the first two, strike at theaters next to each other."

"Any reason you think that's what he's doing?"

"Just a hunch. The fact that this theater is next door to the Von Feurston, and your play is a murder mystery—well, maybe it's my imagination, but the Drummond would seem to be an attractive target for him."

"Maybe an attractive target for the killer, but not an attractive contemplation for anyone involved with *Knock 'Em Dead*."

"No, it certainly isn't. Where was this young man coming from? The guy who bumped into you."

"I don't know. He was just coming down the sidewalk in the opposite direction I was going."

"You didn't see him come out of the alley separating the theaters?"

"No."

"Well, how about that cup of tea?"

"All right, although we'll have to make it quick.

The director has called an extra rehearsal this evening."

"A problem with the show?"

"No, just ironing out some wrinkles."

We'd reached the doors to the street when his beeper went off. He checked the number displayed on the tiny screen. "Sorry, Mrs. Fletcher, but we'll have to postpone the tea."

"That's quite all right."

"We'll catch up again."

"I hope it's just for a pleasant cup of tea and a chat, not about murder."

"Hopefully."

"Detective Hayes."

"Yes."

"Your name is Hayes. Any relation to the great actress, Helen Hayes?"

"As a matter of fact yes. Maybe that's why they gave me this case. We're third cousins twice removed."

"You didn't elect to follow in her footsteps as an actor?"

"Not for a living, but I do act in community theater. Excuse me, Mrs. Fletcher, I have to run."

He left as members of the cast and crew came through the doors, including Pamela South, who'd been hired to replace Jenny Forrest.

"How did the press conference go?" asked

Charles Flowers, who played the detective in the play.

"Fine," I said, my fingers involuntarily going to the rip in my coat.

"Hi, Jessica," Hanna Shawn said. She played the daughter, Waldine, and was alleged to be one of Harry Schrumm's girlfriends. She wore a white T-shirt with KNOCK 'EM DEAD emblazoned on it in red, a gift from Schrumm to every cast and crew member. Although she was older than the character I'd created, and might have been cast because of a personal relationship with Schrumm, she was a wonderful Waldine in my estimation.

"Hi, Hanna. All set for another run-through?"

"No. I had other plans tonight. But the show comes first. It *always* comes first."

I wandered into the theater where the stage was being readied for the rehearsal.

"Has anyone seen Linda?" I asked.

No one had.

"She said she'd be here tonight," I added.

"She'll show up," Cy Walpole said, sounding as though the thought wasn't especially pleasing to him.

"I saw her a half hour ago," a member of the crew offered.

"Great. I'll go find her."

I climbed a short set of steps up to the stage, watched the activity for a few minutes, then went backstage, carefully navigating lighting paraphernalia strewn on the floor, and made my way to a narrow, poorly lit hallway off of which opened a series of tiny rooms and offices. I poked my head into Schrumm's on-site office, then into the tech director's space. Both were empty.

At the end of the hall were the three largest rooms, one devoted to props and costumes, the other two serving as dressing and makeup rooms for the male and female members of the cast. Because *Knock 'Em Dead* was relatively contemporary, costumes in the classic sense were few; the story took place in the late 1940s, which meant only that characters wore clothing appropriate to that decade. The stage door leading to the alley separating the Drummond and Von Feurston Theaters was just beyond and around the corner from the costume and dressing rooms.

"Linda?" I said. The only response was an echo of my own voice.

I proceeded down the hall. "Linda?" I repeated, looking into an office shared by the costume and set designers. No answer.

I took a few steps in the direction of the prop and dressing rooms, which brought me to a section of the hallway where the few bulbs in the ceiling had burned out, creating a dark, shadowy span of twenty feet. I stopped. What was that noise? Someone laughing? I looked up at the ceiling, then turned and peered down the length of the hall. I narrowed my eyes. What was I seeing? It couldn't be. A man's face, chalk white, with blood-red lips, seemed to hover in the air at the hallway's end. He laughed, more a cackle—or was it traffic noise from outside?—then disappeared as quickly as he'd appeared.

I drew a deep breath and reminded myself that I was seeing things, an apparition, my mind playing games with itself. Herbert Spiegel, one of the world's foremost experts on the use of medical hypnosis and a friend of mine, often says that if you tell someone *not* to think of purple elephants, that's all they'll see—purple elephants. The ghost of Marcus Drummond, indeed. I must have been subconsciously thinking of the legend and saw him, my purple elephant.

I laughed, shook my head, and continued in the direction of the dressing and costume rooms.

"Linda?"

As I approached the larger rooms, I noticed that the door to the costume and prop room was partially open. Light from within spilled through the gap and slashed across the hallway floor.

I went to the door, raised my hand to knock, then pressed my fingers against it. It opened slowly, making a grating sound. I stepped inside. The clothing to be worn by the actors and actresses hung from metal garment racks with wheels. There were three of them, one for each act.

I sighed. Linda wasn't there either. The crew member must have been mistaken, or she'd been there and left.

I was suddenly aware of a strong cold breeze coming from outside the room. Someone must have opened the stage door when entering from the alley. Usually, there was a man at the door, an old-timer named Vic who'd been working stage doors, he told me, for more than fifty years. Vic—I didn't know his last name—was a sweet man, obviously mentally impaired to some extent, but whose pleasant personality and dedication to his responsibilities as guardian of the door more than made up for any intellectual deficiencies.

I didn't hear the stage door close, and started to leave the room with the intention of going to see why it remained open, letting in the cold. But as I did, something caught my eye. Shoes worn by the cast members were neatly lined up beneath the rack of clothing for each act. The woman in charge of the room was a stickler for detail and order and had thrown more than one tantrum when someone failed to hang up their costumes with the left-hand sleeve facing out, or had placed their shoes beneath the appropriate rack without having the toes pointing out.

Because everything was so neatly arranged, a

black shoe lying on its side was blatantly evident. I crouched and grabbed it with the intention of setting it right with the others. But it wouldn't move because—because there was a foot in it.

I stood and backed away, then slowly and with trepidation approached the clothing rack again. I was tempted to close my eyes but forced them to remain open as I wheeled one end of the rack into the center of the room. In doing so, I was now able to see the person whose foot occupied the shoe. It was Harry Schrumm, *Knock 'Em Dead's* producer. He was slumped against the wall, the foot I'd grabbed jutting out beneath the rack, his other foot tucked beneath him. I didn't know which was more shocking, the round circle of blood the color of cardinals oozing around the knife in his chest, staining his white shirt, or the macabre scene the killer had created. The soft-brimmed tweed hat worn by the father in the play was propped at a bizarre angle on his head, and the pipe used by the father hung from his slack mouth. His eyes were open; he was looking directly at me as if asking for help.

Too late for that.

I crouched and took a closer look. As I did, the hat fell off, revealing what appeared to be a bruise on his left temple that had been covered by the hat.

I straightened up, drew a breath, took in the

rest of the room, then left it and walked with purpose down the hall, past the empty offices and the dark area where I thought I'd seen the ghost of Marcus Drummond, and to the stage where Cyrus Walpole was about to begin rehearsing a scene from the third act. Everyone stopped and stared at me as I stepped into the middle of the scene.

"Jessica?" Walpole said. "Is there something—?"

"There's been a murder!" I said, surprised at the calm in my voice. "Harry Schrumm. In the costume room. Someone has murdered him!"

Stunned silence.

I looked into their faces. Actors and actresses. A play, a fictitious dramatic performance. Broadway. The stage. All the magic of make-believe. A murder mystery created by me in my imagination.

But the reality of my announcement was all too apparent at that moment.

This wasn't playacting.

This murder was the real thing, real life, real blood, a real weapon that didn't retract into its handle or shoot blanks.

I preferred the fictitious version.

Chapter 9

I don't know who called the police, but they were there within minutes, dozens of them swarming all over the Drummond Theater. The first to arrive were uniformed officers, but Lieutenant Hayes walked in minutes later. I was with the cast, crew, and Cyrus Walpole and Aaron Manley on the stage where we'd been told to remain until further instructed. Hayes disappeared backstage for ten minutes, then reappeared and came directly to me.

"Didn't think I'd see you again so soon," he said.

"I wish you hadn't."

"I understand you discovered the body, Mrs. Fletcher."

"That's right. In the costume and prop room."

"Touch anything?"

"No. Yes. I pulled on the shoe on Mr. Schrumm's

foot to put it in line with other shoes, but I don't think I moved it. And I pulled the costume rack out. That's when I saw him."

"See anybody else in the vicinity?"

"No."

"Did you go out the stage door?"

"No, but it was open."

"How do you know that?"

"I felt cold air coming through it."

"Where was the doorman? What's his name, Vic?"

"Yes, Vic. I don't know where he was."

Hayes looked at the others on the stage. "Anyone have anything to offer before we get down to individual questioning? Anyone see anything?"

Walpole was the only one to respond. "I realize you have a job to do, Inspector, and a nasty one at that, but I have a play to get ready for previews. How long will you be disrupting us?"

I thought Hayes might respond angrily, but he smiled and said, "First of all, sir, I'm a detective, not an inspector."

"And I'm British," Walpole said. "Pardon the misnomer."

"Confucius said that the first step to wisdom is calling things by the correct name. I tend to agree with him."

"Quite," Walpole said.

"Second, the extent of disruption will depend

upon you and your cast and crew, how cooperative you are."

"Why wouldn't we cooperate?" Manley asked. "We didn't kill Schrumm."

Hayes ignored him. "Third," he said, "you're free to continue your rehearsal as long as you can concentrate with officers and forensics personnel climbing over you."

"Maybe we should call it a day," Joe McCartney said.

"Absolutely not," Walpole insisted.

Hayes said to the assembled, "To any of your knowledge, is everyone who was in the theater at the time of the murder present here on stage?"

We looked at each other.

"Where's Linda?" Hanna Shawn asked.

"Who's Linda?" Hayes asked.

"The casting director," Dave Potts said.

"She was in the theater," said the crew member who'd told me the same thing.

"I looked for her but couldn't find her," I said. "In fact, that's what I was doing when I came upon Mr. Schrumm's body; looking for her."

"How many of you saw the deceased here in the theater this afternoon?"

A few people indicated they had, and Hayes questioned them about the circumstances under which they'd seen Schrumm.

"See anybody here in the theater who shouldn't

be here?" Hayes asked. "A stranger? Somebody not involved with the show?"

Denials all around.

"Does anyone know why the doorman, Vic, wasn't at his post?"

Another round of negative responses.

Hayes told his uniformed officers that no one was to leave the theater without his permission, and repeated the admonition to us. He asked Walpole where there was an empty room in which he could begin individual questioning. "That way we'll be out of your hair and you can go on with your rehearsal. I would appreciate it, however, if no one discusses the murder until after I've had a chance to question everyone." Although he put it gently, his voice said it was an order, not a request.

"The theater manager's office is upstairs."

"Is he here?"

"I don't believe so," Walpole said, "but it's open. I went up there myself a little earlier."

"All right," Hayes said, "that's where we'll go. Mrs. Fletcher, would you come with me?"

"Of course."

As we started to leave the stage, an officer stationed at the rear of the theater came down the aisle: "Hey, Detective, there's a guy in the lobby who wants in."

"Who is he?" Hayes asked.

"Name's Factor. He says he owns the show."

"*Owns* it?" Aaron Manley muttered.

"Mr. and Mrs. Factor are the financial backers of *Knock 'Em Dead*," I explained.

"Bring him in," Hayes told the officer.

Arnold Factor, dressed in a tuxedo, strode down the aisle, topcoat over his arm, a white silk scarf trailing behind. "What's this about Harry Schrumm being murdered?" he asked loudly.

"I understand you're the financial backer of the play," Hayes said pleasantly, extending his hand. "I'm Detective Henry Hayes, NYPD." He flashed his badge with the other hand.

"A pleasure," Factor said. "Harry's dead?" He asked the question of me.

"I'm afraid so," I said.

Factor turned to Hayes. "My God, how could such a dreadful thing happen? The Broadway serial killer?"

Hayes shrugged. "We're just beginning our investigation, Mr. Factor. Were you in the theater this afternoon?"

"No."

"Well, now that you're here, I'd like to have a chance to chat with you, learn something about the deceased. As the show's backer, you obviously had a close relationship with him as producer."

"I knew him well. We were involved in a number of theatrical projects."

"Mrs. Fletcher," Hayes said, "would you mind if I spoke with Mr. Factor first?"

"Of course not."

"Mr. Factor," Hayes said, indicating the backer was to follow him up the aisle in the direction of the lobby.

When they were gone Walpole said, "All right, let's get to it. We've got a bloody mess of problems to address, and the bloody previews are two weeks away. Places everyone for act two, scene three. This show must go on—no matter who dies in the process!"

I sat in the darkened theater and watched the rehearsal. There was no doubt that the shock of Harry Schrumm having been murdered was taking its toll on the cast. They seemed to walk through the scenes, all energy drained from them. Frankly, I didn't know how any of them could continue, knowing that their producer's body lay twenty yards away in the costume room.

But that reality was changed when a half hour later, Harry Schrumm's shrouded corpse was carried on a stretcher down the theater aisle and to the street where an NYPD ambulance waited. I turned from it as it passed. Not that avoiding seeing his covered body would spare me any unpleasant memories. All I could see was him propped up against the wall behind the costume rack, eyes wide open, looking almost silly with the hat on his head at an odd angle and the pipe drooping from his mouth.

My attention was then divided between the rehearsal on stage and the work of the police officers and members of the NYPD's forensic unit as they combed the theater for clues. I doubted they'd find anything out there, considering the murder had taken place backstage and that the killer had probably escaped into the alley through the stage door. But they had to cover all bases.

My mind also wandered back to what Detective Hayes had said earlier, that the Broadway serial killer seemed to work in a geographic pattern. Hayes had been right. The killer had chosen a theater adjacent to the scene of his last crime.

Then I reminded myself that I was assuming Harry Schrumm had been murdered by the serial killer. It certainly looked that way, but I'd lived long enough to know that things weren't always as they appeared to be where murder was involved—*especially* where murder was involved.

Still, all signs pointed to Schrumm being the serial killer's fifth victim.

My pragmatic New England side also kicked in. What would this do to the opening of *Knock 'Em Dead*? Despite Cyrus Walpole's determination that the show must go on in grand theatrical tradition, losing one's producer at this late stage had to have an impact. Unless, of course, what Matt Miller said was true, that a producer's only function was to raise money and hire talent. In that case, his work had been completed quite a while ago.

Hayes reappeared, followed by Arnold Factor. "If I'm no longer needed," Factor said, "I'll be going. I'm meeting Mrs. Factor and friends for dinner at Twenty-one."

"Nice place," Hayes said.

"You'll excuse me?"

"Sure," said Hayes.

The detective and I watched Factor leave the theater.

"Interesting guy," Hayes said.

"How so?"

"Made a few stabs at being upset about the producer's murder, but then started talking about how this would boost ticket sales."

"How callous."

"He's right, I guess. The press has surrounded the theater, Mrs. Fletcher. I called for one of our press officers to handle it. I don't suppose you want to deal with them."

"No, I certainly don't."

"Ready for a talk?"

"Of course. By the way, did you examine the body?"

"Looked at it, that's all."

"Did you notice the bruise on his left temple?"

"Yes. Why do you ask?"

"I'm wondering whether he received the bruise after falling from the wound to his chest, or whether he was killed by a blow to the head."

Hayes smiled. "I see why you're a mystery writer."

"Just a naturally curious lady, Detective. I'm ready if you are."

Chapter 10

The theater manager's office was off the small second floor lobby from which two doors led to the balcony. The manager, Peter Monroe, was a prissy little fellow with an array of nervous tics—a twitch in his left eye, index fingers constantly tapping against his thumbs, and a habit of hunching his narrow shoulders against some unseen force. Nervous traits aside, he was a pleasant man who, when not closeted in his small, cramped office, could be seen scurrying about the theater in search of things needing attention. He seemed always to be there; that he wasn't present that day was unusual.

The door was open. Detective Hayes took Mr. Monroe's chair behind the desk, and I sat in the only other chair available, positioning it so I could see Hayes between high piles of paper on the desk.

"Might as well start from the beginning, Mrs. Fletcher," the detective said, pulling out a slender notebook and pen from his inside jacket pocket.

"How do you define the beginning?" I asked.

"I suppose going back to your episode yesterday in front of the theater."

"When I was attacked with that stage prop? There really isn't much to tell about that. A young actress was fired from the play. I happened along when she was arguing with the casting director, Linda Amsted, who'd been handed the unpleasant task of telling her she was no longer a member of the cast. It looked to me—I suppose it looked the same to anyone who was present—that she was attacking Ms. Amsted with a real knife. When I arrived, she shifted her attention from Linda and came after me, ramming the knife into my chest. The blade retracted into the handle the way it was designed to do and that was that."

"Ms. Forrest. Jenny Forrest," Hayes said.

"That's right."

"Quite a picture in the *Post*."

"I had no idea someone had taken a photo. I was surprised to see it on the front page."

"Did Ms. Forrest have a grudge against Mr. Schrumm for being fired?"

"I wouldn't know, although it's reasonable to assume she did. After all, he would have had to approve her dismissal from the show."

"Why was it left to Ms. Amsted to fire her? It's unusual, at least according to my experience, for a casting director to do the firing."

"I thought the same thing. But Linda seems to have an expanded role in the production. She and Harry Schrumm were—well, it's just a rumor but they supposedly were close personally."

"I see," he said, noting it in his book. "You said you were looking for her when you discovered the body. Did you know she was in the theater?"

"One of the crew told me she was, but I never saw her."

Hayes thought for a moment before asking, "Anyone else personally close, as you put it, with the deceased?"

I shrugged. "Just rumors."

"I learned a long time ago never to dismiss rumors. There's often something behind them."

I nodded. "The actress who replaced Jenny Forrest, Pamela South, is alleged to be—was—one of Harry Schrumm's girlfriends. But I emphasize I don't know this firsthand."

"What about the man I spoke with downstairs, Arnold Factor. He's the backer?"

"He and his wife, Jill. They've evidently backed a number of Schrumm's shows."

"Happy investors?"

I thought back to the conversation I'd had with the Factors in the restaurant. "Again, Detective

Hayes, I only know what I've been told. The Factors indicated to me they weren't happy with the way Schrumm was padding the payroll. They said it wasn't unusual for him to do this, that he'd done it with previous shows with which they'd been involved."

"But they keep investing."

"Yes."

"What about others in the cast? Any friction between them and Schrumm?"

I laughed. "There's friction between everyone involved with this play, from what I've observed. I suppose it goes with the artistic temperament and the pressures of putting on a Broadway production."

"I suppose so. The director, the British gentleman? He and the deceased get along?"

"They seemed to. A few minor flaps but nothing more serious than that."

"What about Ms. Larsen?"

"April? She's expressed her disappointment in certain aspects of the show, although she seems to have been most upset with Linda Amsted, at least recently."

"What about her relationship with the deceased?"

April Larsen had termed Harry Schrumm a liar. I told the detective this.

"She goes back a long way with him," Hayes said.

"Does she?"

"Yes. Remember the scandal with her and Schrumm out in Hollywood?"

"No. I don't keep up with showbiz scandals."

"Good for you. I don't remember the details, but I'll check it out. Have you seen the man again who bumped into you on the street?"

"No."

"I'd like to borrow your coat, Mrs. Fletcher."

"Borrow it?"

"Yes. Have the lab examine the cut more closely. I promise to have it back to you within twenty-four hours."

"It's the only warm coat I brought with me."

"Maybe your wardrobe mistress can come up with another. If not, I'll arrange for one."

"All right. I left it downstairs. Anything else?"

"Once again, the circumstances under which you found the body."

I repeated it step-by-step for him, ending with, "It looks as though Harry Schrumm's murder was at the hand of your so-called Broadway serial killer."

"On the surface, yes. Same MO, same pattern. Theaters adjacent to each other. The killing occurred backstage. The killer takes the time to pose the victim in some macabre way. Not a bad bet that Mr. Schrumm has become the serial killer's latest victim."

"I get the feeling it's a bet you're not willing to make," I said.

"I'm a cop, not a gambler, Mrs. Fletcher. If it was the serial killer, you and everyone else connected with *Knock 'Em Dead* can rest easy. The killer will go on to another theater."

Hayes stood, arched his back against a stiffness, and groaned.

"Bad back?" I asked, also standing.

"Yeah. Always tightens up when I'm investigating a murder."

"And loosens up once you've solved one?"

"Exactly. Are you planning on being in New York until the opening?"

"Yes. I'm staying at the Westin Central Park South."

We left the office and went downstairs to the lobby.

"Do me a favor?" Hayes asked.

"Sure."

"Keep your eyes and ears open for me, keep in touch."

"Of course. You'll be questioning the others now?"

"Uh-huh. I'll try to schedule things so that anyone not rehearsing a scene at the moment is next. Your coat?"

We went into the theater where I'd left it on a seat. Hayes put it over his arm and motioned for a uniformed policewoman to join us. "Maggie, this is Jessica Fletcher, the mystery writer. *Knock 'Em Dead* is based upon her novel. She needs a warm coat for a few days. Think you can rustle one up for her?"

"Sure."

I followed Hayes to where Aaron Manley sat talking with Charles Flowers. I introduced Hayes to them.

"Would you please come with me, Mr. Flowers?" Hayes said. The actor followed him up the aisle.

"What did he ask you?" Manley asked me.

"Nothing special."

"It's a waste of time questioning any of us," Manley said. "None of us is the serial killer."

I didn't respond. Although everything pointed to Harry Schrumm being another victim of the Broadway serial killer, I shared Detective Hayes's reticence about coming to that conclusion too quickly.

I wandered aimlessly back in the direction of the lobby and stood in it, looking out through the glass doors leading to the street where the sidewalk was packed with members of the press, uniformed officers, and gawkers. Marked NYPD cars with lights flashing sent spears of light over everything and everybody. Then I noticed a young man who seemed to be arguing with one of the officers guarding the door. The officer saw me and asked, "You're Mrs. Fletcher?"

"Yes," I said.

"This kid claims he's your bodyguard."

I peered through the glass at the face pressed against it. It belonged to a tall, gawky young man with a prominent nose and Adam's apple, a mop of red hair covering his ears and forehead, and wearing what looked like a uniform.

"He says his name is—"

"Wendell Watson," I said.

Wendell smiled and wiggled his fingers at me. I waved back.

"What is he, some nut?" the officer asked.

"No," I said with a deep, resigned sigh, "he's— Please let him in."

After receiving permission from Detective Hayes, Wendell Watson, son of Gloria Watson of Cabot Cove, was allowed to enter the theater.

"Hi, Mrs. Fletcher. Sheriff Metzger sent me to protect you."

I smiled.

"Mom sends her best."

"That's nice."

"Don't worry about a thing," he said. "I won't leave your side. I'm licensed, you know."

"So I've heard. Congratulations."

"Thank you, ma'am. I appreciate that, and I'm pleased to be here."

"And I'm—I'm pleased that you are. Should I call you Officer Watson?"

"No, ma'am. Wendell will be just fine."

"Then that's what it will be. Welcome to New York, Wendell."

Chapter 11

The questioning of *Knock 'Em Dead*'s cast and crew by Detective Henry Hayes promised to last well into the night. I was taken with his demeanor and calm approach. Previous brushes with members of New York's police department had left me impressed with their professionalism but put off by their gruff, at times insensitive manner.

Hayes was a different breed. Perhaps it was his artistic bent that softened his attitude toward the gritty task of solving murders. Maybe it represented a simple determination to improve the image of the New York PD, which had taken so many hits lately because of corruption and bias-generated use of excessive force. Whatever the reason, I liked Detective Hayes and his quiet, polite manner while investigating the murder of Harry Schrumm.

Not that the murder was his alone to investigate. He was joined by his partner in the homicide division, a stocky young man of Mediterranean origins whose personality was as abrasive as Hayes's was affable. His name was Tony Vasile. He had the face of a prize fighter—flat, broad nose, heavy black eyebrows, and a mane of close-cropped black hair that hugged the contours of his head as though it had been painted on.

Did Hayes and Vasile represent the classic good cop–bad cop team? I watched their interaction with interest. After Hayes had questioned someone from the show and allowed him or her to return to the rehearsal, Vasile pulled the person aside and went to another room off the backstage hallway for further interrogation. Judging from the expressions on their faces, time spent with Vasile was considerably more stressful than it had been with Hayes.

Hayes emerged from having interviewed Charles Flowers and sat next to me in the theater. Wendell Watson, whom I'd earlier introduced to Hayes, was in the seat to my right.

"Mind if Mrs. Fletcher and I have a private conversation?" Hayes said to my young protector, who hadn't left my side since arriving.

Wendell looked to me for the answer.

"It's all right," I said. "Why don't you sit over there, Wendell, or get a cup of coffee backstage."

He reluctantly unfolded from the seat and slowly left us, glancing back every few steps, hurt on his face.

"Seems like a nice young man," Hayes said.

"He is, although I'd prefer he not be here, at least not as my so-called bodyguard. Our sheriff back in Cabot Cove, Mort Metzger, sent him. Mort meant well, but I don't think I'll get used to having Wendell tag along everywhere I go."

"Probably can't hurt. Mrs. Fletcher, I—"

"Please call me Jessica."

"Okay. What can you tell me about the casting director, Ms. Amsted?"

"Linda? Nothing, really, just that she has a wonderful reputation in her field and is very nice. I've become more friendly with her than with any other person involved with the play."

"Any idea where she might be?"

"No. At home?"

"We've tried that. No luck. She's not at her office either. An assistant said she was supposed to be here at the theater."

"That was my understanding, too. Are you concerned about her?"

"No, but I would like to speak with her. She seems to have been somewhat pivotal in Schrumm's life."

"I hope she's all right," I said.

A uniformed officer came to us. "Lieutenant,

the woman you've been looking for, Ms. Amsted, just arrived. She's in the lobby."

Hayes and I looked at each other and smiled.

"Send her down," Hayes told the officer.

Linda Amsted arrived flustered and breathless. "I just heard about Harry," she said to me. "I can't believe it."

"Linda, this is Lieutenant Henry Hayes. He's investigating the murder."

Hayes stood and extended his hand. "A pleasure meeting you, Ms. Amsted."

"Oh. What? You're a detective. Who could have done such a thing? The serial killer who's been murdering people on Broadway?"

"That's one possibility we're looking into," Hayes said. "Had you been at the theater earlier in the day, Ms. Amsted?"

"No. Well, I was for only a few minutes. I had an appointment downtown."

"What time were you here?"

"Oh, I don't know. About one, one-thirty."

"How long did you stay?"

"A half hour at the most."

I did a mental calculation. I'd arrived at the theater in time for the four o'clock press conference, and started looking for Linda after it had concluded, which was approximately four-thirty. The crew member said he'd seen her a half hour before that.

"One of the crew said he'd seen you after the press conference ended," I said to her. "I was looking for you when I came upon Harry's body."

I couldn't tell from the look she gave me whether she was surprised, angry, or both.

"He must have been mistaken," she said. "I was long gone by then."

"At your appointment downtown," Hayes said.

"Yes."

"Mind if I ask who you met with?"

"Of course not. Are you suspecting me of Harry's murder?"

"No, ma'am, but I'm questioning everyone involved with this play. I understand you and the deceased were close."

Another sharp look from her.

"You'd worked together professionally before," Hayes quickly added, stressing *professionally*.

"That's right," Linda said. "I'd cast for him a number of times, theater and motion pictures."

It was the second time someone had mentioned motion pictures in connection with Harry Schrumm. Detective Hayes had referred to an incident of some sort between Schrumm and April Larsen in Hollywood, and now Linda brought it up. I didn't know Harry Schrumm's age, but he was undoubtedly older than he'd appeared, thanks to a regimen of personal trainers, hair dye, and tanning salons.

Hayes made notations in his book.

"No, I wasn't here later in the afternoon," Linda said. "As I told you, I had a meeting downtown."

Hayes glanced up at her.

"A meeting with Roy Richardson."

"The acting teacher?"

"Yes."

Another entry in Hayes's notebook.

"What time did you meet?"

"Two."

"The meeting was about?"

"We meet once a month. Roy chooses his most promising students and has them read for me. If I like what I see, they go into my computer for possible future casting."

"You've been with Richardson ever since?"

"No. We met until five. I had dinner after that."

"With Richardson?"

"Alone."

"Where?"

"Looking for a good restaurant, Lieutenant?"

Hayes laughed. "Always."

"The Gramercy Tavern."

"Fancy place for a solo meal."

"I go there often."

"They know you."

"Yes. I suppose you want to know what I ate."

"Only if it was good."

"A chicken Caesar salad, glass of white wine. I

always sit in the front room, the tavern. It's less expensive."

"So I've heard."

Linda's composure when she arrived was frayed, but she'd quickly become calm, and her answers to Hayes's questions had a confrontational edge to them. Now, she turned to me, took one of my hands in hers, and said softly, "What a tragedy, Jess. And you had to be the one to discover Harry's body." To Hayes: "How was he killed, Lieutenant?"

"To be determined by the medical examiner."

"Did the killer leave his usual grotesque calling card?"

I started to reply, but Hayes cut me off. "I'd just as soon not talk about that for the moment, Ms. Amsted."

"Then he did—leave his calling card."

Hayes's partner, Vasile, came from the stage and joined us. Hayes introduced Linda to him. "I think Lieutenant Vasile would like to ask you some questions, Ms. Amsted," Hayes said.

"All right," she said, standing.

"Follow me," said Vasile. He led her down the aisle, up on to the stage, and into the wings.

Hayes chewed on the cap of his pen and narrowed his eyes. I was hesitant to disrupt his thinking, but didn't have to. He said absently, "Roy Richardson."

It took me a second to recognize the name as the person Linda had met with that afternoon.

"The acting teacher," I said.

"Yes. Know of him?"

"No."

"A guru. Thousands of acting students. He built his reputation on using analytic techniques to get his students to open up and use their inner pain and turmoil to enhance their performances."

"Sounds like an interesting approach."

Hayes shrugged. "I took a couple of classes with him years ago, before I became a cop. I thought I'd take Broadway by storm with a few lessons from him under my belt."

"And?"

"The experience convinced me to scrap my acting plans and apply to the NYPD. I hated the classes. As far as I'm concerned, he's a charlatan. No, maybe not. He has had some notable success stories, actors and actresses coming out of his school and doing well. What bothered me was that there was an exploitative aspect to it, all these dreamy-eyed kids waiting tables in order to pay his fees, and having their guts wrenched by him. I had the feeling he enjoyed their pain beyond what it might contribute to their acting technique."

"Sounds charming."

"He's that, too. Every member of the cast I've

questioned studied with him at one time or another."

"Really?"

"I wonder if that's how they ended up in your friend's casting computer."

"Very possibly."

"Well, Jessica—I feel a little uncomfortable calling one of the world's greatest mystery writers by her first name."

"Don't be. I'd be uncomfortable if you didn't."

"I have to get back to headquarters. Tony will stay here. How late do you expect the rehearsal to run?"

"I have no idea."

"Funny," he said to himself.

"What's funny?"

"Ms. Amsted's assistant at her office said she was supposed to be here at the theater. Never mentioned a meeting with Richardson."

He snapped out of his contemplative mood. "The entire theater will be a crime scene and off limits to everyone except those who absolutely have to be here."

"Of course."

Wendell, who'd sat sipping coffee from a plastic cup a few rows away, immediately got up when Hayes did and came to my side.

"I understand you're a licensed security guard, young man," Hayes said pleasantly.

"Yes, sir."

"Looking for a career in law enforcement?"

"Yes, sir. My goal is to become a member of the Cabot Cove police department. Sheriff Metzger already told me I might have a chance in a few years."

"Good for you, son," Hayes said, reaching up to pat him on the shoulder. "Just make sure you take good care of Mrs. Fletcher."

"You can count on that, sir. I won't let her out of my sight for a minute."

I don't know whether my grimace was evident, but I couldn't help it. Hayes smiled at me. "Talk to you later, Jessica," he said and walked away.

The policewoman approached carrying what appeared to be a uniform-issue blue winter coat. "Best I could do," she said, handing it to me.

"It'll be just fine," I said. "Thank you."

Peter Monroe, the stage manager, suddenly appeared carrying a cell phone.

"You're back," I said.

"Yes, and wish I wasn't." His left eye was flickering faster than ever. "You have a call. It's your agent." He handed the phone to me.

"Matt," I said.

"I heard on the radio. You okay?"

"I'm fine."

"Good. Dinner?"

"I—that would be fine except—" I looked at Wendell, who hovered over me.

"Except what?"

"It'll be a threesome."

"Who's the third?"

"My bodyguard."

"Your *what*?"

"My bodyguard. Sheriff Metzger sent him down from Cabot Cove. His name is Wendell Watson. He's licensed."

"Are you in danger?"

"Not with Wendell at my side."

"He has to come with us to dinner? I mean, can't he wait outside?"

"I couldn't do that, Matt. Besides, you should get to know him. He might become New York's police commissioner one day."

"Really?"

"Would you send a car for me, Matt? The sidewalk outside the theater is chockablock with press."

"Sure, and I'll be in it. Give me a half hour."

Chapter 12

Matt took us to dinner at Morton's, a quintessential power-broker steakhouse in midtown Manhattan, where my porterhouse would have fed four back home, and certainly would have resulted in a large doggy-bag. But since the three of us didn't have a dog to take anything home to, the sizable leftovers were whisked away, hopefully as a treat to a dog-owning member of the restaurant's efficient and pleasant staff.

Being there with Wendell Watson made for awkward conversation. It wasn't anything he did or said—he said little during dinner—but there was a natural reluctance on both my and Matt's parts to openly discuss what was happening at the Drummond Theater, especially the potential tangible ramifications of Harry Schrumm's murder. However, Wendell was a smoker, and a polite one. He retreated from the table to the bar a few times to light up, leaving Matt and me to compress our myriad thoughts into short bursts of conversation.

The car that had taken us from the theater to the restaurant waited outside on Forty-fifth Street and returned us to the hotel.

"I understand you'll be staying with your uncle in Brooklyn," I said to Wendell.

"Yes, ma'am, only I don't know how to get there. Mom said there's a subway that goes to Brooklyn. I suppose I'll take that."

"Have you talked to your uncle since arriving in New York?" I asked.

"Nope. Went right to the theater after I got off the bus."

Matt and I looked at each other. The contemplation of this gangly young man who'd never been away from Cabot Cove, Maine, navigating New York City's subway system at night in search of an uncle in Brooklyn was anathema.

"I'd ask you to stay with me," Matt said, "but Susan and I have a one-bedroom apartment. The house in the Hamptons is too far away."

I thought for a moment before saying, "I'll see if the hotel has a vacant room. They seem to be full, but there's no harm in asking." I offered it knowing I'd have to pay for an extra room, but it seemed a small price to ensure Wendell's safety in Manhattan. *Who was protecting whom?*

The Westin's night manager told me they were fully booked, with the exception of a two-bedroom, two-bath suite.

"I'll take it," I said. "Can you have me moved right away?"

"Of course, Mrs. Fletcher. I'll send people to pack you up and bring everything to the new suite. It's right down the hall from where you are now."

I went to where Wendell stood in the lobby.

"You're staying here," I said.

He looked around. "It's pretty fancy, Mrs. Fletcher. I don't have much money with me and—"

"It won't cost you anything. I'm changing my room to a two-bedroom suite."

"Stay in *your* room?" he said, sounding worried. "I don't know if Sheriff Metzger would approve of that."

"You're not staying in *my* room, Wendell. You're staying in *your* room, with your own bath."

"If you say so."

"I say so. I don't want you traveling by yourself at night on the subway. When we get to the suite, I want you to call your uncle and mother immediately, tell them you're safe and that they aren't to worry."

"Okay."

"Would you like something to drink while we wait?"

"A soda would be fine."

"Sounds good to me."

The bar, located off the lobby, was busy, but we found a small table, took it, and ordered a Coke for him, a club soda for me. A TV played silently behind the bar, a basketball game's ten players performing their acrobatics sans sound.

I raised my glass to Wendell. "Well," I said, "here's to your arrival in New York. Sorry it involves murder, but—"

I was looking at him, but the TV was in my peripheral vision. The game was suddenly obliterated by breaking news. A newsman filled the screen while a headline crawled across the bottom of it. I was transfixed, my glass held motionless above the table, the words on the screen telling the tale: Broadway serial killer strikes twice in one day—Two murders at the Drummond Theater— The play, *Knock 'Em Dead*, again the scene of a savage attack—Stay tuned for details at eleven.

"Excuse me," I said, getting up and going to a public phone in the lobby.

I tried Matt Miller first, then Vaughan Buckley, both without success. I was about to call the theater manager's office when I remembered that Lieutenant Henry Hayes had given me his card. I tried the main number listed on it and was connected with headquarters. The officer taking the call was reluctant to give me information, but after I properly identified myself and told him Detective Hayes had asked me to stay in close touch, he told me the detective was at the Drummond Theater, and that he'd contact him by beeper. I gave him the number of the booth from which I'd placed the call.

It wasn't more than two minutes before Hayes called.

"Lieutenant, I just saw a report on TV that there's been a second murder at the theater."

"Leave it to the press to get it wrong. There hasn't been a second murder *at the theater*."

"But—"

"It happened a block away, behind a bar."

"Why would the press say it happened at the theater?"

"Because the deceased is the doorman at the Drummond's stage door."

My sharp intake of breath was audible over the phone, I was sure. "Vic?"

"Right."

"That lovely old man?"

"Yes, that lovely old man. Somebody hit him in the head in an alley behind the bar."

"How horrible."

"I just came from there. He'd been drinking since late afternoon."

"That seems out of character," I said. "He didn't seem the sort of man who would abandon his post to go drinking."

"I wouldn't know. The press is all over the street here. How are things at the hotel?"

"Quiet. I—"

I looked through the doors to the street where media vehicles mingled with police cars. A number of men and woman, all from the press I assumed, were being kept from entering by the night manager and some of his staff.

"Maybe not so quiet," I said. "Will you be at the theater tomorrow?"

"Sure will. You?"

"Yes."

"Good. I'll be there at ten."

"And so will I. Thanks for the update."

"I'd say it's my pleasure, but that would be a lie."

The night manager spotted me, crossed the lobby and said, "We have you moved, Mrs. Fletcher. You can go to the suite any time."

"Thank you."

"I think you'd better go now. See what's happening outside?"

"Yes, I do. Let me get Wendell."

"Wendell?"

"My bodyguard. He's from Maine."

"Oh."

I paid for our soft drinks and brought Wendell back out to the lobby.

"This is Wendell," I said to the night manager.

"Pleased to meet you, sir," Wendell said, his head bobbing.

"Wendell will be staying in the suite with me."

"Your bodyguard."

"Yes."

"I'm from Cabot Cove, Maine," Wendell said.

"He's licensed," I said.

"Of course. This way, please."

The suite was perfectly configured. The second, smaller bedroom was physically separated from the living room and my bedroom by doors.

"You go ahead and call your uncle and mother," I told him once we were inside. "And get to bed. We have an early start tomorrow."

"Yes, ma'am."

It suddenly occurred to me that he didn't have any luggage.

"Do you have fresh clothes with you, Wendell?"

"Yes, ma'am, except I left them at the theater."

"Oh, well, we'll have the hotel send up a toothbrush and other necessities. You'll just have to sleep in what you're wearing. You can change tomorrow once we get to the theater."

"Okay," he said, then headed for his end of the suite. He stopped, turned, and said, "I guess you don't like having me around, Mrs. Fletcher, and I can't say that I blame you. But the sheriff said it was important that you be safe here in New York." His grin was pleasant and genuine. "I'll just do my job and try to stay out of your way."

"Wendell," I said, "I am very happy you are here with me in New York. I feel safe and protected, thanks to you. The sheriff and the others in the theater party will be arriving next week and we'll all have a good time enjoying New York City."

"That sounds fine. Mrs. Fletcher?"

"Yes."

"How come they call it the Big Apple?"

I smiled. "Because you can taste life here with one bite like no other place on earth. Good night, Wendell."

"Good night, Mrs. Fletcher."

And taste murder, too, I thought after he'd closed the door and I was alone.

Murder!

An unwelcome intruder into my dream of having one of my books turned into a Broadway play.

Chapter 13

Wendell and I had breakfast at seven and headed directly for the theater. The second murder of someone connected with *Knock 'Em Dead* and the Drummond Theater was again front page news, as expected. But the press corps that had camped in front of the hotel earlier in the evening evidently had been called to cover bigger and better stories—bigger and better murders? Only a few stragglers were in front of the Westin when we climbed into a cab.

The scene on West Forty-fourth Street was a different matter. TV remote trucks were parked in front of the theater, their telescoping antennas jutting up like church spires, the religion of fast-breaking news. Reporters hurled questions at me as I exited the cab but I ignored them, answering only with a smile and wave of my hand. As we reached the front doors where two uniformed officers stood guard, a young woman asked, "Is it true you had a bodyguard brought in from Maine because you're afraid for your life?"

I turned and faced her. "Of course not," I said.

"Then who's he?" she asked, indicating Wendell, wearing his green security guard's uniform.

"He's—just a friend." To Wendell: "Come on. Let's get inside." He looked as though he was about to respond to the reporter.

One of the officers was reluctant to allow us to enter, but Lieutenant Hayes's partner, Tony Vasile, spotted me from the lobby and waved us inside.

"Good morning," I said.

"Good morning, Mrs. Fletcher." He looked at Wendell but said nothing.

"My friend, here, left his suitcase at the theater overnight. He needs to get it."

"Where did you leave it?" Vasile asked.

"In there," Wendell replied, indicating the theater itself.

"What did it look like?" Vasile asked.

Wendell shrugged. "A big old thing. It's my mom's. She let me use it for the trip."

"Cloth? Green? With yellow flowers?"

"Yes, sir, that's it."

"It's at headquarters."

"How did it end up there?" I asked.

139

"Bomb squad took it."

"Bomb squad?"

"Couldn't take any chances. You see a strange suitcase standing alone and you think bomb."

"I suppose so," I said. "Can we arrange to have it returned?"

"I'll see what I can do."

We followed Vasile into what's called the house, where hundreds of theater goers would enjoy *Knock 'Em Dead* in less than two weeks—provided the show wasn't cancelled.

"Lieutenant Hayes said he'd meet me here at ten," I said once we'd reached the stage apron. A lone technician fiddled with lighting equipment. Other than him and the police, we seemed to be the only ones there.

"Yeah, he'll be here by then."

Two uniformed officers emerged from backstage. One asked Vasile, "When's our relief coming?"

"Any minute," Vasile said.

The officers muttered something unintelligible and disappeared into the wings.

"I take it they're securing the area where Harry's murder took place," I said.

"That's right."

"I heard about Vic, the doorman. Anything new on that front?"

"No."

"He was killed behind a bar a block from here?"

"That's right. Somebody whacked him on the head."

"How sad. He was such a nice man."

"I wouldn't know, but he shouldn't have been off drinking and leaving the door unmanned. Maybe if he hadn't, Schrumm would still be alive."

"What's the name of the bar?" I asked.

"Rafferty's. Down the street."

"Was it a robbery gone wrong?" I asked.

"Could be. His wallet was gone."

"What do people in the bar say? How long had he been there?"

"What are you doing, getting information for your next murder mystery?" he asked unpleasantly.

"No, not at all," I replied. "Just natural curiosity."

The theater manager, Peter Monroe, arrived.

"When will you and your people be gone?" he asked Vasile. "I'm getting nothing but complaints from the director and the producer's office. We have a play to put on."

I expected an angry response from the detective. Instead, he said nothing, just walked away shaking his head.

"You mentioned the producer's office," I told Monroe. "Who has taken over the production from Mr. Schrumm?"

141

"Mrs. Factor."

"Mrs. Factor? She's one of the backers, not the producer."

"I just know what I'm told," Monroe said. "She called and said she and her husband are the producers now that Schrumm is gone."

"I'm not doubting you," I said. "Is it unusual for a backer to become the producer under such circumstances?"

His laugh was small and rueful. "I wouldn't know," he said. "I've never been involved in 'such circumstances.' Excuse me. I've got to deal with ticket sales."

"Not an especially pleasant fella," Wendell said.

"He's under a lot of pressure," I said. "Everyone is. What we have to do is get you some clean clothes in case the police won't release your suitcase."

Wendell smiled. "Imagine that, Mrs. Fletcher, thinking there was a bomb in Momma's suitcase. That's pretty funny."

I didn't see much humor in it at the moment.

"Wendell," I said, "here's two hundred dollars." I handed him ten twenty dollar bills. "I want you to go out, find a men's store, and buy yourself some fresh underwear, a few shirts, socks, things like that. The hotel was good enough to provide you with a razor, toothbrush, and other necessities."

"I couldn't do that, Mrs. Fletcher."

"Couldn't do what?"

"Take your money to buy me clothes."

"I insist. Make sure the officers at the front door know who you are and that you'll be coming back so they'll let you in."

"If you say so, only I shouldn't be leaving you alone, not even for a minute."

"I'm perfectly safe here, Wendell. There are police everywhere."

"Sheriff Metzger told me not to trust the police in New York. He said they're corrupt."

"Most of them aren't, Wendell, just a few bad apples like any other group. Go on, now."

He ambled from the house and to the lobby, passing Lieutenant Hayes, who'd just arrived. The detective greeted me warmly.

"I almost dreaded getting up," I said, "facing another day and another murder."

"Unfortunately, you get used to it, Mrs. Fletcher, if you do it enough. Where's your young friend going?"

"To buy clothes. You confiscated his suitcase from the theater."

"That was his? Didn't have any choice."

"I understand. Lieutenant, about the doorman, Vic. What was his last name?"

"I've been asked that a lot. No one seemed to know, if he did have a last name. Was known as

143

Vic by everyone for years. We got it from Monroe, the theater manager. Victor Righetti."

"A family?"

"Can't find any. Lived by himself in a residence hotel on the Upper West Side."

"I understand he'd been at the bar drinking all afternoon. Rafferty's is the name of it?"

"Right. A Broadway institution. Been around for years. Never any trouble there. Owned by the same Irish family for generations."

"Did you interview other patrons, or the staff?"

"Not personally, but others did. I haven't seen their report. Actually, I didn't catch that case. I'm strictly full-time on the serial killer."

"And you don't think there's any connection?"

"No. Entirely different MO. The old guy's wallet was missing. Hit over the head. I don't see any linkup."

"I suppose you're right. I just heard that the Factors, the show's backers, have taken over as co-producers."

His eyebrows went up. "Really? When did that happen?"

"Must have happened right away. Mr. Monroe told me he received a call from Mrs. Factor informing him of it."

"The body's not even cold yet."

"I suppose it's a matter of the show having to go on."

Cyrus Walpole and Aaron Manley arrived.

"Dreadful thing, what happened to Vic," Walpole said. "Another victim of the serial killer, Lieutenant?"

"No. Unrelated."

"A robbery victim?"

"Appears that way."

"I hate to say it," Manley said, "but I'm glad it was just a robbery. I've reached an age where I read the obits every day. When I see someone my age has died, I always hope it was from some motorcycle accident, or a fall from a mountain. I don't want to know about death by natural causes."

"What did you know about Vic?" Hayes asked the two men.

"Nice chap," Walpole said. "Quiet. Pleasant."

"He gave me the creeps," Manley said.

His comment surprised Hayes and me. "Why do you say that?" Hayes asked.

"He had a funny look about him. You know, he had that one eye that didn't open all the way."

Hayes ignored the statement and asked, "Either of you know why he left the stage door?"

They shook their heads.

"He ever do it before?"

"I wouldn't know," said Walpole. "I don't keep track of the stage door. I have a play to whip into shape. Speaking of that, Lieutenant, I've called a rehearsal for noon. Any chance you and your people will be finished up and gone by then? Your presence is unnerving to the cast and crew." He looked at me and said, "I had to beg Hanna to stay with the show. She's convinced that if she comes to this theater, she'll end up like Schrumm. Dave Potts has expressed similar fears."

"I'd think having the police here would help allay those concerns," I offered.

"No offense, Lieutenant," Manley said, "but I'd like to see you gone, too. I have rewrites to do. I can't concentrate with a bunch of cops around."

Hayes, ever calm, said, "I'm as anxious to be out of here, Mr. Manley, as you are to have me gone. We're moving as fast as we can, believe me."

"It can't be fast enough," Manley said, walking away.

"You'll have to excuse my friend," Walpole said. "He's a writer, and we all know what they're like." He smiled. "With Mrs. Fletcher an obvious exception."

"No need to exclude me, Cy," I said, smiling sweetly.

"I have work to do," Walpole said, and left.

"Everyone's a little high-strung," I said as the homicide detective and I sat next to each other.

"Mind going over how you discovered Mr. Schrumm's body again?" he asked.

"Not at all, although I don't think I forgot anything the first time around."

I went step-by-step, from the moment I left the stage in search of Linda Amsted until pulling out the costume rack and finding Harry Schrumm.

"That's it?"

"Yes. Well, no, there is one other thing I neglected to mention."

"Oh?"

"I saw the ghost of Marcus Drummond."

"Did you now?"

"Of course, it really wasn't a ghost. It must have been something the light created—you know, an interplay of light and shadow."

"But it looked like Marcus Drummond?"

"Yes, but only because I must have been subconsciously thinking of him at that moment. The old purple elephant syndrome at work."

"I'm not familiar with that."

I explained.

"Interesting," he said. "Any chance what you thought was a ghost was actually a person—maybe the person who'd just killed Harry Schrumm?"

"I don't think so."

"Just a thought. Oh, by the way, the lab examined your torn coat. It *was* cut, with a very sharp knife with a serrated blade."

"Then it wasn't an accident."

"No, I think not. I had one of our people take it to a tailor. You should have it back this afternoon better than new."

"That's very kind, but you didn't have to go to that trouble," I said. "I sort of like the uniform issue you gave me."

"No trouble at all." He stood. "You'll be here for the rehearsal?"

"That's my plan, although I thought I might skip out for lunch."

"Have you spoken with Ms. Amsted?"

"No."

"I plan to see her again this afternoon, at her office."

"Have *you* spoken with Jenny Forrest?"

"Your attacker? Yes. Last night. I imagine she's a wonderful actress."

"I thought so."

"Not your most stable of young women, however."

"No argument from me."

"Keep a confidence, Mrs. Fletcher?"

"I'm pretty good at that."

"We may have a break in the serial killer case."

"That's wonderful news."

"I can't be specific, but Mr. Schrumm's murder might have provided the evidence we need."

"Something to do with the knife used to kill Schrumm?"

"No. It was clean. No prints. It evidently came from the small kitchen backstage. Its handle matches the rest of a set in there."

"Well, I hope you solve it soon. I don't blame the cast members who are afraid to come to work. Having a madman running around killing people in Broadway theaters is unnerving, at best."

"See you later."

I wondered why he'd not only chosen to share that information with me, but why it had come immediately following his comments about Jenny Forrest. It was a fleeting question because things became busy in the theater. The cast and crew drifted in over the next half hour, each cleared by police manning the doors to the premises. Wendell returned shortly before noon carrying shopping bags.

"Successful shopping trip?" I asked.

"I guess so. Things sure cost more here in the Big Apple than back in Cabot Cove."

He showed me his purchases, which he'd made at a discount men's store on Times Square. At least he had some clean clothing in the event he never saw his suitcase again.

"Hungry?" I asked.

He grinned. "I always am, Mrs. Fletcher. My mother says I eat more than any ten people she knows."

I would have preferred to leave the theater

alone, but knew that would be impossible, not with Wendell Watson's heightened sense of duty.

"Let's go get some lunch," I said, standing. "I know a wonderful Irish pub just a block away."

Chapter 14

Although it was only a few minutes past noon when Wendell and I entered Rafferty's, the bar and restaurant were crowded. We were greeted by a pretty young redheaded woman wearing a Kelly green T-shirt with RAFFERTY'S in white across her chest. Lilting Irish music came from speakers behind the bustling bar.

"Two for lunch?" she asked.

"Yes," I said, "but we'd like to have a drink at the bar first."

"All right. I'm afraid all the tables in the back are taken, but you can have that one over there in the corner. It'll be ready in a few minutes."

"Fine, thank you."

There were two available bar stools at the long, scarred wooden bar manned by a beefy, red-cheeked gentleman wearing a green apron with the bar's name on it over a white shirt and green tie. The moment we settled on our stools, he was in front of us.

"What's your pleasure?" he asked.

"Wendell?"

"Just a Coke, please."

It might have been a wince that came over the bartender's broad face, I couldn't be sure.

"You, ma'am?" he asked.

"Ah, club soda with a slice of lime."

As he went to fetch our drinks, Wendell leaned close to me and whispered, "I'm not sure I should be in a bar wearing my uniform. I'm on duty."

"As long as you don't drink anything alcoholic, I'm sure it's all right for you to be here. After all, this is where I am, and you're supposed to be with me."

"That's true," he said, obviously relieved.

Rafferty's was a spirited place, with conversations running up and down the bar. Our drinks were served, and I sipped while tuning in on what was being said on either side of me.

". . . and it had to be robbery," a man said between swallows of a dark beer in a large mug. "Poor old bastard had all that money on him. Must have talked too loud."

"That's the way I figure. Had to be somebody here who heard him, saw the wad he laid on the bar."

"Nice old guy, huh?"

"Sure was."

"Excuse me," I said, "but I couldn't help over-hearing what you were saying. You're referring to what happened to Vic Righetti last night."

"Was that his name? Never knew his last name. Always called him Vic. You're a friend of his?"

"Yes, a good friend. You obviously were here with him yesterday afternoon."

"Yes, we were," the second gentleman said.

"You knew Vic from here?" I asked.

"Knew him from lots of places. He's—he'd been around Broadway for years. Sort of a fixture, I suppose you'd say. Been tending stage doors as long as I can remember."

"Yes, I know," I said. "Strange, wasn't it, that he left the stage door at the Drummond to come here. Not like Vic."

One of the men laughed. "We kidded him about being here earlier than usual. He always came in on his supper break, around five. Surprised to see him wander in when he did."

"Did he say why he was here earlier than usual?"

"The money the man gave him," said the other customer.

"What money?" I asked. "What man?"

They looked at each other and shrugged. One of them said, "All Vic said was that the man—

yeah, that's what he called him, 'the man'—gave him a couple of hundred dollars to leave for a few hours."

"Did he say why he was given the money?"

"I don't think so."

"Yeah, he did," said the second customer. "Something about needing to meet somebody."

"Vic was meeting someone?"

"No, the man who gave him the money was. You never really understood everything Vic was saying. He was, you know, kind of slow, didn't always say things right."

I leaned back on the stool, cupped my glass of club soda in both hands, and digested what I'd heard. As I sorted through it, one thought dominated. The man who gave Vic money to vacate his post at the Drummond Theater had to have been someone Vic knew—knew well—and furthermore was someone in power. I couldn't conceive of Vic abandoning the stage door for money from a stranger, or even someone with whom he was familiar but who did not have the authority to make such a request.

Who could that be?

I immediately thought of Harry Schrumm. That scenario played for me. What if Schrumm had planned to meet secretly with someone, paid Vic to absent himself for a few hours, met the visitor, and was killed by that person?

On the flip side, it might have been Schrumm's murderer who paid Vic to leave the stage door in order to enter the theater unobserved and kill Schrumm.

Those possibilities led me to silently question what Schrumm had been doing in the costume and prop room. I'd never seen him there, although I certainly hadn't been observing his comings and goings with any regularity. I made a mental note to ask Lieutenant Hayes whether it was possible that Schrumm had been killed elsewhere, and brought to the costume room by his murderer, perhaps to more easily stage the bizarre setting for the body.

I also intended to ask Hayes whether previous murders by the so-called Broadway serial killer involved a missing doorman. If so, that would certainly lend credence to the serial killer having taken Harry Schrumm's life, too.

Wendell had sat silently during my exchange with the other customers. I turned to him and asked whether he was ready to take our table. Before I could, the bartender, who'd obviously overheard the conversation, leaned his elbows on the bar and asked, "Are you some sort of cop?"

My look of surprise faded into a smile. "No," I said, "I'm just a friend of the man who was killed last night behind your bar."

"I've told the cops everything I know." He looked at Wendell: "You a cop?"

Wendell grinned. "No, sir, but I intend to be one some day. I'm a security guard right now, assigned to protect Mrs. Jessica Fletcher."

"That so?" said the bartender. To me: "Are you Jessica Fletcher?"

"Yes."

"You write books, murder mysteries."

"That's right."

"I don't read much but I know your name. Hey, isn't that your play going to open at the Drummond?"

"Yes. In less than two weeks."

"The serial killer got your producer, too. Harry Schrumm."

"Did you know him?"

"Sure." He looked left and right and said in a conspiratorial tone, "Hate to say anything bad about the dead, but he was no prince, I'll tell you that."

I chose to ignore the unkind comment. "The Factors are producing my play now."

The bartender screwed up his face in thought before saying, "Right, that husband and wife team that backs shows. Always on the society pages, attending some fancy party or another. I heard they're living way over their heads."

"I hadn't heard that."

"Yeah. A lot of my customers are theater people, not the weirdos but crew types, union workers. One of their union delegates comes in here all the time. He told me last week the Factors have more lawsuits against them than the president. I love people like that. They live the high life and stiff everybody they do business with. A couple of bartender friends of mine work in pretty fancy places. The Factors run up big bills, throw big parties, then toss the bills in the garbage. 'So, sue me' is what they say. Hell of a way to live. Another Coke, officer? You, ma'am?"

"I think we'd better eat. That's our table over there."

"Kelly will put the drinks on the bill. Enjoy."

I dropped a dollar tip on the bar, and we sat at the table.

"Seems like a nice fella," Wendell said, his eyes dancing over the menu.

"Very nice. I think I'll have the Irish stew."

"I never had that before," Wendell said. "I don't like things all mixed up together. I'll have a hamburger."

"Good. And then we have to get back to the theater. There are a few questions I'd like answered."

Chapter 15

The first person I saw when we returned to the theater was Priscilla. She was in the lobby. I was surprised she hadn't shown up earlier, considering the frenzy of media activity over the two murders.

"How are you?" I asked.

"Couldn't be better. I know that sounds ghoulish, but it's also reality. Dead bodies aren't my thing, but since we now have two of them—no fault of mine—and the press wants to treat the murders as front page news—again, no fault of mine—I have no choice but to deal with it. I've been in my office fielding requests for you to appear on TV. *The Today Show*, *Good Morning America*, *CBS Morning*, *Larry King*, *The Tonight Show*—the list is endless."

"I hope you told them I'm not available."

"Of course I did. Well, I did leave the door open in case you decide to accept one or two. You know, just selected shows, the biggies."

"Hmmm."

"Here's today's papers," she said, handing them to me. "It's still page one."

I'd kept up with what the press wrote about Harry Schrumm's murder. Fortunately, no photograph of the crime scene had been released to the media, sparing him the loss of dignity such a picture would have engendered, sprawled up against a wall wearing a silly hat, a pipe suspended from his mouth. Stories I read mentioned that the killer had propped a hat and pipe on the deceased, but didn't identify them as being part of the show's props and costumes. The bruise on his temple wasn't mentioned in any of the reports I saw; cause of death, even though it hadn't been officially released, was a stab wound to the chest.

The theater manager, Peter Monroe, joined us. He was considerably more animated than I was accustomed to seeing.

"Ticket sales are strong," he said, "v-e-r-y strong. Sold out for three months."

"That's wonderful," I said, meaning it, yet reticent to express joy that people were snapping up tickets to see my murder mystery because of *real* murders.

"People are reserving as much as a year ahead," he added.

"It's a guaranteed hit," Priscilla chimed in.

"Is Detective Hayes in the building?" I asked, changing the subject.

"He was here a few minutes ago," Monroe said. "Backstage."

"Excuse me." I left them and ascended to the stage where the rehearsal was in full swing. A uniformed officer kept people from going into the wings. Wendell walked in lock-step with me.

"Is Detective Hayes back there?" I asked.

"Yes, ma'am."

"May I go back and see him?"

"No, ma'am."

"Would you please get him for me?"

He responded by backing up a few steps and shouting to an unseen officer: "Tell the lieutenant there's someone out here to see him." Cy Walpole glared at us for interrupting, sighed, shook his large head, and continued giving directions to the actors and actresses.

Hayes appeared a minute later, and we retreated to the house seats.

"How was lunch?" he asked.

"Fine. We went to Rafferty's."

A knowing smile crossed his lips. "I figured you would."

"You did? A nice place, very friendly. The food was good."

"Glad to hear it."

"Got a minute?"

"Sure."

I said to Wendell, "Would you see if you can rustle me up a cup of tea?"

When he hesitated, Hayes said, "It's okay, son. I'll make sure nothing happens to Mrs. Fletcher while you're gone."

"I have a couple of questions," I said once Wendell was out of earshot.

"Shoot."

"Is there any possibility that Schrumm's body was moved to the costume and prop room after being killed elsewhere?"

"No. Forensics thoroughly covered that possibility. He was killed where you found him. Why do you ask?"

"Because I was curious why he'd gone to that room. I'd never seen him there before, which proves nothing, of course. It's the room closest to the stage door."

"Yes, it is. Next question?"

"With any of the previous serial killings, was a doorman missing when one of them occurred?"

He rubbed his chin. "I don't believe so. No, that wasn't the case in any of the previous murders."

"Thanks."

"What did you find out at Rafferty's?"

"Find out? What makes you think I wanted to find out anything?"

"Because I figure you wouldn't have gone there unless you wanted to ask questions. That seems to be your nature."

I laughed. "I suppose it is. What did I find out? Let's see. Vic Righetti went there earlier than usual because someone he described as 'the man' gave him two hundred dollars to abandon his post at the stage door. This unnamed man, according to a few pleasant fellows at the bar who were with Vic yesterday, supposedly wanted to meet someone secretly, either in the alley behind the theater, or just inside the stage door."

"You don't know the man's name?"

"No, although it could have been Harry Schrumm. Maybe the person he was meeting is the killer."

"Go on."

"According to the bartender at Rafferty's, Harry Schrumm wasn't an especially popular person. And, again according to the bartender, Mr. and Mrs. Factor have a habit of not paying their bills."

Hayes grinned. "You found out a lot."

"All hearsay."

"And confirmed by people I talked to at Rafferty's."

"Oh?"

"All except the scuttlebutt about the Factors. Patrons we questioned are assuming it was someone at the bar who killed Vic. He was evidently flashing the two hundred dollars he'd been given to get lost."

"I heard that theory, too. Maybe the Broadway serial killer hangs out in Rafferty's."

"Everybody's got to be someplace, as the saying goes. But Vic wasn't killed by the serial killer. As I said, the MO is completely different."

"There's another old saying."

"Which is?"

"People can change, including their MOs."

"Not in this case."

"You're the expert. One more question?"

"As many as you like."

"Why did you take me into your confidence about a possible break in the serial murder case?"

"Did I?"

"Yes, you did."

"Oh, right. I don't know. I suppose I consider you part of my investigating team, Mrs. Fletcher, considering your preeminence in the world of murder mysteries, and the fact that you discovered Schrumm's body. And, I might add, you seem to be asking all the right questions."

"Thank you for the compliment. Care to extend your trust in me?"

"How?"

"Tell me what the break in the case is."

"Can't do that at this moment." He made an exaggerated point of looking around, leaned close, and said, smiling, "In due time—partner. Excuse me."

I watched him retreat into the wings and settled in a seat to observe the rehearsal. It didn't seem to this untrained eye to be going very well. Tempers flared. Walpole totally lost his composure and began screaming at the cast, causing a few of them to storm off the stage, Pamela South, Jenny Forrest's last-minute replacement, in tears.

Walpole then turned his wrath on the playwright, Aaron Manley.

"These bloody changes you keep coming up with have thrown off the entire rhythm of the production. You keep making changes for the sake of making them, damn it, and I want you to stop!"

Manley, who'd been sitting at his laptop computer making additional revisions, jumped to his feet and crossed the stage to Walpole. "Don't you blame the writing for how lousy this play is going, you fat, no talent, British slob!"

Walpole closed the gap between them even further; they now stood six feet apart. Walpole's face was vivid red; his rotund body shook. Manley held one hand behind him, as though ready to throw a punch.

I ran down the aisle to the stage apron.

"Please," I said, "everyone calm down. This will accomplish nothing."

My presence brought members of the cast back to the stage, led by the star of *Knock 'Em Dead*, April Larsen. Everyone started talking at once, hurling insults at one another, cursing, voices rising in pitch until the Drummond Theater reverberated with dissonant, hysterical threats.

I climbed the short set of stairs at stage right, placed myself in the midst of them, held up my hands, and summoned my loudest voice: *"Stop it!"*

There was immediate silence.

"You're acting like petulant children," I said.

"He is," Walpole said, pointing at Manley.

Manley cocked his fist and snarled.

"Put your fist down," I said to the playwright.

He looked as though he might hit me.

"Down!" I said.

Joseph McCartney, who played the father, quietly applauded.

I broke into a nervous smile.

"You're right, Jessica," David Potts said. "This is no way to get a play ready for Broadway."

Charles Flowers, raised his hand. "I have an idea. Why don't we all sit down with Jessica and have a good old-fashioned, soul-searching talk. Vent our frustrations. You're the voice of reason,

Jessica. Willing to play shrink to a group therapy session?"

"I don't know, I—"

"That's a ridiculous suggestion," April Larsen said. "Are we professionals or not? Group therapy! Good Lord."

"I like the idea," Dave Potts said. "When can we do it?"

"No time like the present," McCartney replied. "The rehearsal's not going anywhere. Let's order in food and hash it out." He swiveled to take in the others' reactions. April Larsen left the stage, followed by Brett Burton, the pensive actor playing the older son.

"The hell with them," Flowers said. He turned to the assistant director, Wade Agus. "Order in some food, Wade, and wine. This might go on into the night."

Agus looked to Walpole.

"Oh, go order some bloody food," Walpole said. "This rehearsal's a disaster anyway."

"Maybe we should call Linda Amsted," Pamela South said. "She could use some head shrinking."

"I'll call her," Hanna Shawn offered.

"Maybe our new producers ought to be here, too," Walpole said. "Now that Harry's dead, we all work for them."

Linda Amsted hadn't been on my mind lately, but now that her name had been mentioned, I wondered how things had gone with Lieutenant Hayes's further questioning of her. I was able to ask because he appeared just then, apparently lured by the commotion.

"What's going on?" he asked me.

"I got your tea, Mrs. Fletcher," Wendell said. "I left it down there."

"What? Oh, thank you, Wendell. Any scones or biscuits around?"

"Scones?"

"Something sweet to go with the tea. Please?"

He walked away.

"He takes guarding you seriously," Hayes said.

"Yes. He's a sweet boy. I know his mother."

"Sounded like a real ruckus," Hayes said.

"Artistic temperaments rising to the surface. We're about to have a group therapy session."

He looked puzzled.

"A chance to vent frustrations. Did you meet with Linda Amsted again?"

"No, although I did interview Roy Richardson."

"Who's he?"

"The acting teacher."

"Oh, right, I'd forgotten his name. Linda said she'd been with him at the time of Schrumm's murder."

"Richardson confirms it."

"That's a relief."

"Why?"

"Because I'd hate to think that Linda might be involved. I really like her."

"Her office says she had to fly to Los Angeles on a last-minute casting job. I should have told her she was to stay in New York until the investigation is completed. Slipped my mind."

"I'm sure it doesn't matter."

"I suppose not. I have the hotel she's staying at in L.A. if I need to speak with her. You should meet him."

"Meet who?"

"Roy Richardson."

"From the little you told me about him, I'm not sure I'd want to."

Hayes laughed. "Maybe I shouldn't have said what I did. He trained everyone in this cast."

"So you mentioned."

"I arranged for you to attend one of his classes tomorrow."

"I—"

"I know I should have asked you first, but I was there and it seemed an opportune moment. You'll enjoy it. Or at least find it interesting."

I cocked my head and looked at him quizzically.

His smile was amiable. "I'd like to know what you think of Richardson and his methods."

"I'm hardly the one to judge. I'm not an actress."

"But you are observant. Eleven tomorrow morning? I lied a little. I told him because your play was about to open, and because the cast had trained with him, you'd expressed a keen interest in his classes."

"Don't you mean that *you* have a keen interest in his classes, or, more accurately, *him*?"

"You'll go?"

"Of course. Any other little white lies I should be aware of?"

He shook his head.

"Then I'd better get ready to lead the group therapy session."

We'd no sooner parted, he returning to the wings, I heading for where most of the cast and crew had congregated on stage, when Jill Factor strode down the aisle with purpose. She wore a severely cut gray pantsuit, a red beret that might have come from the Israeli army, and carried a large briefcase obviously stuffed with something, presumably papers. She stopped in front of the stage, dropped the briefcase to the floor, placed her hands on her hips and asked in a loud, authoritative voice, "What's going on here?"

Cy Walpole came to the stage apron. "The rehearsal was going poorly so we—"

"I suggest the rehearsal resume immediately and that it begin to go smoothly. We have previews in nine days. Every seat is sold. The critics will be here ready to find every fault they can. Let's go. You've wasted enough time."

Walpole flushed crimson, started to say something, turned, and said to the cast, "Places!"

"What happened to getting together to talk?" Joe McCartney asked.

I came to where Jill stood, hands still on her hips. "We were going to sit down and hash a few things out," I said. "There seems to be tension that's getting in the way of rehearsals."

She looked at me as though I'd committed a serious social blunder. "These are supposed to be professional actors and actresses, Jessica. They can deal with their tensions on their own time."

"I was just suggesting that—"

"If you'd like to hash things out, as you put it, I suggest we do it tonight, at our apartment. I assume you're free for dinner."

I was, although I was tempted to say I had plans. I don't deal especially well with people who wear their arrogance on their sleeves.

"Yes, I'm free."

"Good. Seven-thirty. You have the address."

She turned from me and barked another series of orders at Walpole and the cast: "I want to see Act Two." To Aaron Manley: "That scene between the mother and the older son is dreadful. The original version was better. Go back to it."

Manley's look was venomous.

Since I'd been dismissed by her, I wandered away, sat for a few minutes, and watched the rehearsal resume, then decided to go back to the hotel and relax until my command performance at the Factors' penthouse apartment. I considered saying good-bye to Lieutenant Hayes and Priscilla Hoye, but decided not to bother.

Most of the press corps had left their hopeful stakeouts in front of the Drummond, and Wendell and I were able to easily exit the theater, walk half a block, and hail a yellow taxi.

The driver turned to hear where I wanted to go.

"The Westin Central Park South."

He pulled away from the curb.

"No," I said, "I've changed my mind. The Library of Performing Arts at Lincoln Center."

Chapter 16

New York's Lincoln Center for the Performing Arts is internationally known as a vast complex serving as the city's cultural center, but not as many are aware of its splendid library, a rich and deep repository of materials on the popular arts—stage, screen, TV, radio, and related media.

I'd used the library a few years ago when researching one of my novels. The story was set in contemporary Hollywood, but I needed some history of the early days of film. The Lincoln Center library gave me far more than I could ever have used.

"May I help you?" a research librarian seated behind a desk asked when Wendell and I approached. Her strange look at him undoubtedly had to do with the green uniform he wore.

"I believe you can," I said. I turned to Wendell.

"Would you be a dear and find a good magazine or book to read while I take care of business?"

He looked around.

I pointed to a corner of the large room containing tables and chairs and a large rack filled with magazines. "Sit over there for a few minutes."

"All right," he said, ambling off.

I said to the librarian, "I'm researching two people who worked in Hollywood a few years back, the actress April Larsen, and a producer named Harry Schrumm.

Her eyes went up. "*The* Harry Schrumm, who was just murdered?"

"That's right."

"You're Jessica Fletcher."

I nodded.

"He's—was producing *Knock 'Em Dead*, your book."

"Yes, he was, and Ms. Larsen is starring in it."

"What a dreadful thing that happened to him. The Broadway serial killer again."

"It looks that way."

"And you need information on him for a memorial service?"

"Ah, yes. That's right."

"How is April Larsen taking it?"

"His death? Not well."

"They were so close."

"Were they? I mean, yes, they were."

She smiled. "That was quite a story. I was surprised they ended up working together again on your play."

"Time heals all wounds," I said. "I'm sure you have material on their Hollywood days together."

"Of course. All the clips. Let me get you started."

I left the library an hour later with a manila envelope stuffed with copies of newspaper and magazine clippings about Schrumm and April Larsen, individually and collectively. Although neither had achieved the level of salacious celebrity to generate major articles about their earlier relationship in Hollywood, there was plenty to chew on.

When we reached the hotel suite, I broke the news to Wendell that I'd been invited to a private dinner party, and that he couldn't accompany me. He protested at first, but soon realized coming with me was out of the question.

"Why don't you stay here in the suite for the evening, Wendell, order up something you like from room service, and relax. I'll come straight back from dinner. I'll check in from time to time to let you know I'm okay."

That seemed to satisfy him.

I showered, dressed for the evening, and took some time to go through the material from the library before leaving for the Factors' apartment. Naturally, the focus of the articles was on April Larsen, whose movie acting career at the time most of the pieces were written was at what could be termed a pivotal point. Schrumm was a fledgling producer who probably wouldn't have generated much attention if he hadn't become romantically involved with April, the star of his breakthrough picture, *A World Apart*.

According to reviews I'd photocopied, the film was dismal. One especially vicious reviewer summed up his reaction in a single line: "*A World Apart* opened last night. Why?"

That film seemed to mark April Larsen's downward career spiral and struck the death knell in what had been a brief fling between actress and producer. It culminated in April bringing a lawsuit against Schrumm for, among other things, siphoning money from the production budget, resulting in an inferior film, and for "deliberately and callously attempting to ruin her professional career." It was settled out of court, details sealed under the judge's order.

Interesting, I thought, how they ended up together again for *Knock 'Em Dead*. I suppose I was right; time does heal all wounds, at least those particular wounds.

The final few stories about Harry Schrumm reported that he'd left Hollywood for New York where he began producing plays. He was quoted: "I prefer the artistic freedom and dynamic creative atmosphere of Broadway to the Hollywood mill that cares only about the bottom line. Broadway is where I belong."

I was certain there had been other stories about him since his arrival on the Great White Way, but I wasn't interested in those. I'd accomplished at Lincoln Center what I'd set out to do, learn about the previous relationship in Hollywood between Harry Schrumm and April Larsen that Detective Hayes had alluded to. I didn't have any practical use to which to put my newfound knowledge, but I felt better possessing it.

"The Factors' apartment, please," I told the doorman in the marble lobby of their high-rise building on Manhattan's east side. He called up, then told me to take the elevator to the penthouse level.

Arnold Factor, dressed in an obviously expensive English-cut blue suit, white shirt, and muted red-and-blue tie, answered my ring. "So glad you could make it on such short notice," he said, standing back to allow me to enter. The entry foyer was stunning in its size and simplicity, floor and walls gleaming black-and-white marble, the modern furniture copper and brass and glass.

"Come, have a drink," he said, leading me to

the living room, where a woman dressed in a black uniform and white apron delivered a silver tray of canapes to a long bar.

"Thank you, Mary," Factor said to her. To me: "What's your pleasure, Jessica?"

"White wine?"

"Of course. French or California?"

"Either."

"Lately, we've been partial to California wines," he said as he busied himself behind the bar. "They've come quite far with their vineyards, although a good French will ultimately win out. Don't you agree?"

"I hadn't thought about it," I said, "but I'll defer to your experience."

He poured wine for me and mixed a martini for himself. I watched the ritual he went through, first filling a wide cocktail glass with ice cubes and adding water, then putting ice and a drop of vermouth in a stainless steel cocktail shaker, adding gin, and methodically stirring it. He placed a strainer over the top of the shaker, emptied the glass of the ice and water, and carefully poured from the shaker into the glass.

"You seem very much at home making a martini," I said.

"I pride myself on how I make them, Jessica. Today's young people have bastardized the martini, using vodka and a whole array of other inappropriate ingredients. They even have chocolate martinis, for God's sake. There's only one way to make a martini and that's the way I make them. Sure you won't join me?"

"Too potent for me. Where's Mrs. Factor?"

"Getting dressed. She had a tough, eye-opening day at the theater." He came around from behind the bar and raised his glass. We touched rims. "To salvaging *Knock 'Em Dead*," he said.

"I didn't realize we were in the midst of a salvage operation," I said.

"Unfortunately, we are. Please, sit. Take that chair. The view is better."

He was right. From that vantage point, floor-to-ceiling windows afforded a dazzling panoramic view of Manhattan.

"It's even nicer from the terrace," he said, "but not in this weather."

I laughed. "I'm quite used to winter, Arnold, coming from Maine."

"Usually, we've gone south by this time of year. We have a house in Palm Beach. But with the demands of the play, it was out of the question."

I'd taken one sip of my wine when Jill Factor suddenly appeared from the recesses of the apartment wearing a floor-length green silk dress cut low, and accented by an exquisite diamond necklace. My thought at the moment was that if this couple was having financial difficulties, they certainly didn't live as though they did. Of course, I'd known a few people in my life who managed to live far above their means, seemingly always able to juggle what money—and credit—they had to put on a facade of easy wealth. If that was the case with the Factors, they were very good at it.

"Sorry I ran late," she said, coming over to where I sat and extending her hand. "The rehearsal was dreadful, and I stayed later than I'd planned. I see you have a drink. Arnold couldn't entice you into one of his martinis?"

"No," I said, laughing. "The wine is fine."

"The usual?" Arnold asked her.

"Yes."

He went behind the bar again, and Jill took his chair. "I thought you might stay longer at the rehearsal than you did," she said to me. "I could have used some input from you."

"No, I had other things to do. You said it was a dreadful rehearsal. Are things that bad? Previews are just a few days away."

"I'm well aware of that," she said, sighing and accepting a glass from her husband containing a brown liquor and ice. He'd made himself another drink, too, and I had the impression the martini he'd had upon my arrival wasn't his first of the day.

"To opening night," she said.

"Yes," I said, "provided there is one. From what you say, that might be in question."

"Oh, no," Arnold said, standing behind his wife and placing a hand on her bare shoulder as though about to pose for a family portrait. *"Knock 'Em Dead* will open as scheduled, won't it, dear?"

She replied without looking up, "If I have anything to say about it—and I do!"

"Now that you're the producer," I said.

"Tragic what happened to poor old Harry," Arnold said, pulling up a matching red-and-gold Oriental chair. "We're still in shock."

"You knew him a long time," I said.

"Oh, yes, a very long time," said Jill. "It's bad enough when a friend of long-standing dies of natural causes, but when he's slaughtered by this madman, the Broadway serial killer, it's especially hard." Her eyes misted.

"Disgusting, really, the way this nut goes about it," Arnold said, draining what was left of his drink. "Bad enough he goes around killing people, but he has to add his little signature touch by costuming the body. Sticking a pipe from the show in poor old Harry's mouth is sick, really sick."

"There isn't much question, is there, that it was the serial killer?" I asked.

"I should think not," Arnold said. "Open-and-shut."

"I'm not sure I should be telling you this," I said, "but I've heard the police have a break in the case."

"In Harry's murder?" Jill asked.

"In the serial killer case, which includes Harry." They looked at each other.

"That's good news," Arnold said. "More wine?"

"No, thank you."

"Excuse me." He went to the bar to freshen his martini.

"How do you know this, Jessica?" Jill asked.

"Just scuttlebutt. I'm not even sure who said it."

"Someone from the police, I assume."

"I suppose so. This wine is lovely. California?"

"French," Arnold said, stirring his second or third drink.

"We've never even mentioned Vic Righetti," I said.

"Who?" was Jill's response.

"The doorman at the Drummond. He was killed, too."

"I heard about that," Arnold said, rejoining us. "I forgot to mention it, Jill."

"I knew about it. It was the talk at the theater this afternoon."

"Nothing to do with Harry's murder," Arnold said. "A simple robbery."

"A deadly robbery," I said.

Jill made a sound of disgust, stood, went to the window, and wrapped her arms about herself. She said to the glass, "Enough about murder, unless it has to do with the play." She turned and smiled. "I hope you like rack of lamb, Jessica. It's on the menu tonight."

The dining room table was long and lavishly set for three; it could accommodate sixteen. We were served by their housekeeper and cook, Mary. After she'd delivered our salads and gone to the kitchen, Jill said, "It's so difficult finding good help these days. She's the third one we've had in a year."

I silently wondered whether the others had left because they hadn't been paid, if the bartender at Rafferty's was right about the Factors' financial situation.

It was a pleasant if somewhat stiff dinner. The conversation was dominated by talk of *Knock 'Em Dead*, most of it coming from Jill Factor. Arnold, who'd had another martini before dinner, showed the effects of the gin, although I wouldn't characterize him as drunk, just an occasional slurring of a word and a look of fatigue not caused by the hour.

It was over dessert that the topic turned to me.

"I understand you're widowed," Jill said.

"Many years."

"Never interested in marrying again?"

I was uncomfortable being asked such personal

questions by people I hardly knew and didn't particularly like, but I didn't intend to make an issue of it.

"No, I haven't met the right man yet."

"Your husband must have been very special," Jill said.

"He certainly was."

Arnold laughed. "We did some research on you, Jessica."

It was my turn to laugh. "Research? On me?"

"We like to know as much as possible about the people in whom we're investing," said Jill.

"That sounds reasonable. Did you come up with anything about me I should know?"

"Quite a career," Arnold said. "How many books?"

"I've lost track. Dozens."

"And every one a bestseller."

"I wish that were true," I said. "Some of the earlier ones never made the lists, but the reviews were always good, and my publisher is a throwback to an earlier period when authors were nurtured, their careers built over a period of time. I was lucky in that sense."

"How much does a really successful book earn—you know, one that hits the *Times'* bestseller list and stays there?"

I shrugged. "Hard to say. It varies."

"Millions?" Jill asked.

"Some books, but not mine. Let's just say I haven't missed any meals."

They laughed politely. Arnold said, "I read in some gossip column a year or so back that you were romantically involved with a Scotland Yard inspector."

"Did you?"

"Yes."

"I think it's wonderful that a rich and famous murder mystery writer would fall in love with a Scotland Yard type," Jill said.

The conversation was beginning to nettle me. I said, "One, I may be famous but I don't consider myself rich. Two, the gossip columnist you read has it wrong. The Scotland Yard inspector in question and I are good friends, that's all."

"I didn't mean to offend you," Arnold said.

"Why don't we have our coffee and after-dinner drinks in the living room where we can enjoy the view," Jill suggested.

Arnold mixed himself another martini. Jill accepted a balloon snifter of brandy from him; I was content with coffee.

Arnold said from behind the bar, "We'd like to make you a business proposition, Jessica."

"Oh? What might that be?"

"A chance to invest in your own show," Jill said, "to reap the profits of what will obviously be a long-running smash hit."

"I don't understand," I said. "I've already made my investment by writing the book the play is based upon."

Arnold came around the bar and perched on a stool. "Jessica, the percentage of the profits you hold won't amount to much. The real money is the return on financial investment in the show. Jill and I are willing to sell you a half interest in our percentage, which, I hasten to add, is substantial."

Before I could respond, Jill said, "We're willing to sell you fifty percent of our share for only five-hundred-thousand dollars. That's less than half of what we've put up for *Knock 'Em Dead*."

I couldn't help but smile. The last thing I expected was to be given a pitch on investing in the play. I shook my head and said, "I appreciate the offer, but investing in a Broadway show isn't on my agenda."

"Even your *own* Broadway show?" Arnold asked.

"From what I've seen, *especially* my own show."

"Perhaps you'd consider the same stake for, say, four-hundred and fifty thousand?" Jill offered.

I stood. "This has been a lovely evening. The dinner was as wonderful as the views, but I really must be going. May I use your phone?"

"Of course." Arnold pointed to a small study off the living room.

I dialed the hotel and was put through to the

suite. "Wendell, it's Jessica Fletcher. I'm just leaving and should be there in twenty minutes."

"I was getting worried about you," he said.

"I'm just fine. Couldn't be better. See you in twenty minutes."

Arnold stood at the front door holding my repaired coat, which had been returned to me earlier in the day. He helped me into it, saying, "Give it some thought, Jessica. We'll hold the offer open for you for forty-eight hours. Then I'm afraid we'll have to sell to others, who, I might add, are chomping at the bit for the opportunity to grab a piece of this show. We preferred to keep it in the family but—"

"Again, thanks for a lovely evening—and the offer. But I don't need forty-eight hours. I'm much too conservative an investor to be dabbling with Broadway productions."

The telephone rang.

"Where's Mrs. Factor?"

"She wasn't feeling well. A sudden headache."

"Please thank her for me, and tell her I hope she's feeling better."

As he opened the door, I heard Jill Factor say in an angry voice from another room, "So, sue me!" She slammed down the phone.

"Good night," I said.

"Good night," he said.

Chapter 17

I was happy to see Wendell when I walked into the suite. I'm one of those fortunate people who is quite comfortable on my own. Being alone, and being lonely, aren't synonymous with me. But there was something pleasant about being greeted by his grinning face and expressions of concern.

He'd ordered up a hamburger platter, a double order of French fries, a chocolate milk shake, and cherry pie a la mode. There wasn't a morsel of food, or a drop of shake, left on the rolling serving cart.

We talked for a few minutes until I announced, "I have some reading to do before I get to bed. See you in the morning."

"Oh, Mrs. Fletcher, there were some phone calls for you." He handed me paper on which he'd listed them. Seth Hazlitt and Sheriff Mort Metzger were among the names.

"Had a nice chat with the sheriff," Wendell said. "He asked how it was going and I said just fine. He told me I was doing a good job."

"Because you are."

"The sheriff and Dr. Hazlitt heard all about the murders, Mrs. Fletcher. They're real worried even with me here. They said to call them back tonight no matter how late it got."

"I'll do that right now."

"Oh, and some policeman delivered my suitcase to the room. I've got all my things back."

"That's wonderful. See you in the morning."

I closed the door that segregated the living room and my bedroom and bath from his and called Mort Metzger at home.

"From all the news, Mrs. F, it sounds like there won't be anybody left to be in your play."

"Of course there will be."

"Not if that Broadway serial killer keeps murdering people."

"He seems to have slowed down," I said, wishing it were true.

"I heard about that doorman who was killed. Some detective—I think his name was Hayes—said on TV that his murder wasn't by the serial killer. That true?"

"It looks that way, Mort."

"Well, we'll all be down to see you in New

York in a few days. In the meantime, don't let Wendell lose sight of you."

"I won't. Best to Maureen."

When I reached Seth, he said the Broadway serial killer had been dominating the television news from Portland and Bangor. The fact that a local citizen, me, was currently involved with a Broadway play, and that the theater in which it was being rehearsed had been the scene of the latest murder, enhanced the coverage.

"Joe Reedy from the Bangor station called just this morning. He wants to send a crew down to New York with us when we come to see the play. He wants to interview you."

"I suppose I can't stop him, but I could do without TV interviews."

"I understand. How is the play goin', Jessica? All ready for the previews and opening night?"

"Some rough spots, but I think it will shape up. The backers of the show, Arnold and Jill Factor, are now the producers. They offered to sell me half of their interest in *Knock 'Em Dead* for a half million dollars."

"Did they now? I assume you said no."

"Of course I did."

"Worst investment in the world," he said. "Remember when Sue Marshall and her husband, Bill, bought shares in that musical a few years back? Lost everything they put in."

"I remember. Seth, is everything set for the group to come to New York?"

"*Ayuh*. Day after tomorrow."

"I'm really looking forward to it."

"So are we. What do you have planned for tomorrow, Jessica?"

"An acting lesson."

"An acting lesson? You? Are you plannin' to play a role in your play?"

"No, but I thought I ought to see how the actors and actresses in *Knock 'Em Dead* were trained. They all studied with a teacher named Roy Richardson. He's supposed to be very good."

"I'm glad you'll be away from that theater for a spell. No telling when that madman might strike again."

"Not to worry with Wendell here."

"How's that working out?"

"Fine. He's a very nice boy. I have some reading to do, Seth, and then to bed. Can't wait to see everyone."

I waded through the clippings from the library until after midnight when I climbed into bed and turned out the light. I looked forward to attending Roy Richardson's acting class in the morning, not because I was seeking insight into how actors and actresses are taught, but because Lieutenant Hayes wanted me to go there.

Why?

Chapter 18

Roy Richardson's acting studio was on the Upper West Side of Manhattan in what appeared to be a converted warehouse, or factory. A sign to the left of the door read THE RICHARDSON STUDIO.

I was to be there at eleven; it was ten-thirty when I arrived. I stood with Wendell across the street and watched the comings and goings. A steady stream of men and women, mostly young but with some older persons included, streamed through the door or congregated outside laughing and smoking. It looked very much like the exterior of any schoolhouse during recess, the only difference being the age of the students.

I would have preferred to visit the studio without Wendell at my side, but knew it would be fruitless to object to his accompanying me.

At ten of eleven we crossed the street and entered the building. For some reason, I thought the studio of a leading acting teacher would be bright and modern. To the contrary, the large entry hall was drab and poorly lighted. Yellow linoleum on the floor was dirty and torn in places. The paint on the white walls wasn't in better shape. There was a stairway to the left leading down to a basement and up to a second floor. Directly in front of me were double doors that were open, revealing an auditorium and a stage. I estimated there to be a hundred students, most of them seated in the auditorium while others milled about on the stage or in the lobby.

As we entered the auditorium, I observed the stage where students gathered about a man I assumed was Roy Richardson. He looked older than I'd anticipated, although that probably had more to do with the fact that his hair was grayer than his chronological age. He wore his hair in a long ponytail that fell over the back of a billowing white shirt. Jeans and boots completed his attire. He was talking with considerable animation to those around him, laughing loudly at things he said, twisting his slender body to physically enhance his words. The students seemed to be enjoying what he was saying, judging from their laughter.

Wendell and I slipped into aisle seats in the third row. I'd no sooner gotten comfortable when

Richardson shielded his eyes from the lights with his hand, focused on me, and bounded down a short set of steps, hand extended.

"Jessica Fletcher," he said. "Welcome."

I stood and took his outstretched hand. "You undoubtedly are Roy Richardson."

"I was when I got up this morning. The detective said he'd see if you were free today to sit in on one of the classes. I'm delighted you could find the time."

"The pleasure is mine," I said. "I've never attended an acting class before, and I understand you're among the city's best teachers."

He adopted a pose and expression that feigned modesty. "Don't say that," he said, "or I might start believing it."

"What will happen in the class this morning?" I asked.

"The usual. Certain students have been assigned scenes to learn for today, and they'll perform them."

"Sounds like fun. I understand you've trained virtually all the actors and actresses in *Knock 'Em Dead*, the play based upon my book."

"True. You have a talented cast—provided the so-called Broadway serial killer doesn't wipe them out."

"A horrific thought," I said.

"Know what I've been thinking?"

"What?"

"You'll appreciate this, being a mystery writer. I keep wondering whether the serial killer is someone I've trained, some actor or actress, probably a very talented one but with a serious mental illness that's contributed to his or her acting ability."

"Interesting thought," I said.

"In a sense, I'd almost enjoy it if that were the case. You know, the mad acting teacher creating Manhattan's murderous Frankenstein. I'd enjoy the publicity. I've lost students lately and could use an infusion of new blood, if you'll pardon the pun."

I smiled. "That's one thing none of us needs now, new blood. Don't let me keep you from your class. It looks like you've got a lot of students anxious to get started."

"Can't keep the little darlings waiting," he said. "Free for lunch?"

"As a matter of fact I am."

"Good. The class runs until one. Can you hold out till then?"

"I think so."

He looked at Wendell. "Are you supposed to be here?" he asked.

"He's with me," I said. "He's a friend."

"Sure."

Richardson returned to the stage and sat in a tall director's chair with THE TEACHER stenciled across its red canvas back. A matching chair was occupied by a young woman with long black hair wearing jeans and an orange sweater. She held a clipboard. She and Richardson talked for a minute before she shouted, "All right, let's get started. Calm down. Come on, knock off the talk."

The students settled into seats and conversation ceased.

"Molly St. James and Dirk Browder. You're up."

The persons belonging to those names came to the stage and stood before Richardson.

"You're doing *Streetcar*," Richardson said.

"Right," the actor said.

"You're playing Mitch, she's Blanche."

"Yup."

"Ready?"

The actor and actress looked at each other and smiled, drew deep breaths, and launched into the scene. I was familiar with the scene from Tennessee Williams's classic play and leaned forward, my arms on the back of the chair in front of me. I was impressed with what I saw, but Richardson obviously wasn't. He left the chair, arms raised, and said loudly, "You're supposed to be playing characters from Tennessee Williams, not Gilbert and Sullivan. You're showing about as much emotion as Al Gore. Jesus, haven't you gotten anything from these classes?"

The actor and actress looked sheepishly at the stage floor.

Richardson's volume rose in concert with the nastiness of his tone. He berated the two students unmercifully, going so far as to criticize the girl's appearance and the man's masculinity. I winced at every word. Why would anyone, I wondered, subject themselves to such cruel treatment—and pay for the privilege?

Richardson eventually returned to his chair and the students started the scene again. Their approach this time was markedly different from their initial attempt. Frankly, I thought it was better the first time, but Richardson felt otherwise. Not that he praised them. The ensuing half hour was filled with his invective and insulting tirades. I was as relieved when it was over as I was sure the students were.

A second pair was called to the stage and performed a scene from Arthur Miller's *The Crucible*. It was more of the same, only this time the actress didn't have the control of her emotions the way the first actress did. She started sobbing under Richardson's barrage of personal insults and eventually ran from the stage. Richardson laughed and said to those of us in the audience, "That's the first honest emotion I've seen this morning. If she could only apply it to her acting, she might stand a chance of becoming an actress instead of a pathetic wannabe waiting tables in some greasy spoon and wondering why she never made it." He turned to the woman with the clipboard: "Next!" Then, as an aside, "If I can live through another amateur performance."

I considered leaving. I abhor cruelty of any sort, to any living thing, whether it's a four-legged or two-legged species of the animal kingdom. At home, I keep a thin piece of cardboard and a paper cup handy to capture a moth or other insect that's found its way inside, to release it outdoors. Roy Richardson was, to my mind, a sadist, someone who reveled in the power he held over these aspiring people, and who enjoyed their pain.

But the announcement by Richardson's assistant of who was next to perform kept me solidly in my seat.

"Joe Eberly and Jenny Forrest, you're next."

The actor and actress ascended to the stage carrying their scripts. Eberly was a handsome young man who looked as though he could be a model for a military recruiting poster. Immediately behind him was the familiar face of Jenny Forrest, the original younger son's girlfriend, Marcia, in *Knock 'Em Dead*, and my attacker in front of the Drummond Theater.

Richardson's demeanor with this pair was decidedly different than it had been with the previous two, especially with Jenny. He was actually pleasant and kind in the way he addressed her.

After Richardson had delivered a series of compliments about Jenny's performance two weeks ago, he asked, "Ready to give us some Albee?"

"No," Jenny said. She wore the same simple long black dress she'd worn at Linda Amsted's open audition for *Knock 'Em Dead*. It had been designated by Cyrus Walpole as her costume in the show. Familiar large, round glasses sat low on her nose.

"No?" Richardson said, laughing.

"We've changed our minds," Jenny said. "There's a scene from a show that hasn't opened yet we'd like to do."

"Which is?" Richardson asked.

"*Knock 'Em Dead*, the murder mystery opening at the Drummond."

I sat back as though pushed. Why would she decide to use *Knock 'Em Dead* as a vehicle for her class performance? Did she know I was there, perhaps knew I'd be coming before I ever got there? Was this some warped attempt at humor?

"Interesting choice," Richardson said, glancing at me. "We happen to have with us this morning the author of the book on which the play is based, Jessica Fletcher." He pointed to me; some of the students applauded.

"That doesn't matter," Jenny said. "She didn't

write these lines. The playwright, Aaron Manley, did." She looked down at me and smiled, or was it an angry, pointed, twisting of her thin lips?

"All right," Robertson said, "go to it."

They played a scene from the first act in which they profess love for each other, with the character, Marcia, admitting to Joshua her self-loathing. Things look bright for them, until a few scenes later the father is found murdered in the attic following a birthday party for him attended by a dozen people other than the immediate family.

It was a short scene, no longer than six minutes. The other students applauded; so did Roy Richardson. As unsettling as seeing Jenny Forrest again, and having her choose a scene from my play, had been, at least Richardson hadn't berated them.

Before the teacher could give his critique, Jenny came to the stage apron, peered down at me and said, "See what you lost, bitch!" With that she was gone.

Students in the auditorium looked to me for my reaction. I didn't have one. I was too shaken to come up with anything except a blank expression and an inner struggle to keep from shaking.

If the incident had rattled Richardson, he didn't show it. His assistant simply called up the final pair of students for their performance. I sat through their scene, still trying to make sense out of what had happened and occasionally looking over my shoulder to see if Jenny Forrest was in the auditorium. She was so deranged, in my opinion, that I feared she might come up behind me and physically attack me again, maybe this time with a real knife.

She didn't. The class ended with Richardson hurling invective at the two students who'd just performed, then leaving the stage and coming over to me.

"Ready for lunch?" he asked. "I have another class at two, but there's an Italian place around the corner that's pretty fast."

"Would you mind if I take the proverbial raincheck, Mr. Robertson? I just remembered an appointment I have uptown."

He shrugged. "Sure. What did you think?"

"About the class? It was—interesting. Did you know Ms. Forrest would be reading a scene from *Knock 'Em Dead*?"

"No. But then again, Jenny is always full of surprises."

"Like what she said to me when she finished the scene?"

He laughed. "That's Jenny. Being fired from *Knock 'Em Dead*'s cast sent her over the edge. Typical. Open a dictionary to the word volatile and there's a picture of Jenny Forrest to illustrate the meaning. Ignore it. She's a hell of an actress. If she ever gets her personal life together, she'll accomplish great things in theater."

"I don't doubt that. You've been very kind to allow me to sit in. I appreciate it."

"Any time. How's *Knock 'Em Dead* going now that Harry Schrumm's out of the picture?"

"Just fine. Did you know Harry?"

"Sure. He was on my list of people I wouldn't want to sit next to on a long plane trip, but your new producers aren't any better."

"The Factors?"

"Yeah. Lowlifes living the high life."

"I understand Linda Amsted gets to see your most promising students."

"That's right. She was here when Harry got it. She left at five. I told the cops that."

"So I heard. Was Jenny Forrest one of the special students Linda got to see perform?"

"I don't remember. Yes, she was. A year or more ago. You sound like the detective who was here. By the way, he took a few of my classes a while back. Was going to be an actor but decided a steady check from the NYPD made more sense. I agree. He didn't have any talent. He probably makes a better cop."

It was obvious that Roy Richardson had few kind words for anyone, except Jenny Forrest and, I assumed, Linda Amsted.

"I have to get to that appointment," I said, extending my hand. "Thanks again."

"My pleasure."

Wendell and I started to walk up the aisle.

"Mrs. Fletcher."

I turned. "Yes?"

"Watch out for the Broadway serial killer." He laughed.

"I intend to, Mr. Richardson."

"And if he's one of my students, I hope he gives a good performance at his arraignment. My reputation will be on the line."

I left the theater and breathed in the fresh outside air. It was a warm day for February, the sun shining brightly, a clean, bracing scent in the air.

"Boy, he's weird," Wendell said as we headed east.

"He certainly is different," I agreed.

"People shouldn't talk to other people like that," Wendell said. "My mom always says that if you don't have something nice to say to people, you shouldn't say anything."

"Good advice," I said, picking up the pace.

"And that woman swearing at you. I was ready to go up and . . ."

"And what?"

He grinned and shrugged. "Tell her to apologize, I guess."

"You've had a good upbringing, Wendell," I

said, pushing a button supposedly to cause the traffic light to change, but as I've always suspected, being nothing more than a placebo to placate pedestrians to make them feel they're exercising some sort of control.

The light changed.

"Where to now?" Wendell asked as we stepped into the street.

"The Drummond Theater, Wendell. As they say in the theater, the show must go on."

Chapter 19

NYPD Lieutenant Henry Hayes and his partner, Tony Vasile, were at the theater when we arrived. The cast and crew were in the midst of a lunch break; large platters of cold cuts brought in from a local delicatessen had been laid on a table stage left. I was glad to see it. The brisk walk from Robertson's studio to the Drummond had worked up an appetite.

"How was your morning with Robertson?" Hayes asked after I'd made a turkey and Muenster sandwich and poured myself a Diet Coke. Wendell had dug in and retreated to a corner of the auditorium with an overflowing plate.

"Fascinating."

"He's a character."

"He's a sadistic character," I said. "The abuse he heaped on the students performing scenes was distasteful."

"Did he mention me?"

"Yes. He said you were very talented."

Hayes laughed. "No, he didn't," he said. "He probably told you what he told me at my last class, that I was a no-talent jerk with as much chance of making it as an actor as he has of becoming an astronaut."

"He's cruel."

"Worse than that."

"Why did you want me to go there?" I asked between bites of sandwich.

"Just thought you'd find it interesting."

"I have a feeling you had another reason, Lieutenant."

He flashed a boyish grin. "What was your evaluation of him physically?"

"Physically? I'm not sure what you mean."

"Look like anybody you know?"

"No. Average looking, height, weight. Slender build. Gray hair worn in a long, thick ponytail to make him appear younger than he is. Nondescript clothing. Big smile, when he chooses to display it. Very verbal. Jenny Forrest did a scene while I was there."

"One of his pet students."

"How do you know that?"

"Just what I hear. Did she perform well?"

"Yes." I told him of her nasty comment to me at the end of her performance.

"She's nuts."

"Undoubtedly."

I took note that the yellow crime scene ribbon keeping people from the backstage area where I had discovered Harry Schrumm's body had been removed.

"Feel like revisiting the scene of the crime?" Hayes asked.

"All right."

I left my half-eaten sandwich on a seat and followed him backstage to the hallway leading past the offices and to the prop and costume room, dressing rooms, and stage door. Being there again created an eerie feeling, bringing back memories of that day when I walked the hall in search of Linda Amsted. The bulbs above the shadowy twenty-foot section were still out, and that dim, gloomy stretch of hallway was as unpleasant as I remembered it.

"This is where I saw the ghost of Marcus Drummond," I said lightly.

"Wearing a hat and smoking a pipe?" Hayes asked.

"Wearing a—? No. Is he supposed to?"

"That's the way they found him all those years ago, very dead, and with a hat on his head and a pipe in his mouth."

"A hat and a pipe," I said flatly. "Harry Schrumm

was wearing a hat and had a pipe in his mouth when I found him."

"The same hat and pipe used by the actor playing the father in your play."

"You aren't suggesting some strange, psychic connection, are you, between the murders of Marcus Drummond and Harry Schrumm?" I said.

"No."

He stopped. "How about retracing your steps the day you found Schrumm, Jessica."

"All right. Let's see. I looked in this office first, I think. This was Schrumm's office."

"Looked in it for Linda Amsted."

"Correct. This next office belongs to the tech director. I checked it, too."

"And after that?"

"I approached the three large rooms at the end of the corridor, the two dressing rooms, and the prop and costume room."

We went to them.

"I noticed that the doors to the dressing rooms were closed, but the door to props and costumes was cracked open. That's why I decided to go into it."

This time, the door was wide open, and we entered. "The shoe was under this costume rack," I said. "I reached down to straighten it—see how all the shoes are lined up so neatly?—and realized

207

there was a foot in it. That's when I moved the rack and discovered Harry Schrumm."

Hayes pulled on his nose and grunted.

"The hat the killer had propped on his head fell off while I was looking at him. That how I noticed the bruise on his temple."

"Which killed him," Hayes muttered.

"It did? He was killed by a blow to the head?"

"According to the medical examiner. He was dead when the knife was shoved into his chest."

I sat on a low stool used by the seamstress when adjusting costumes for the cast.

"What does that tell you, Jessica?"

"It tells me that the motive for killing him is different than if the knife had been the cause of death. Ramming a knife into someone is, I think, a more deliberate act than hitting someone on the head. Not always, of course, but in general. You plunge a knife into someone's chest with the intent to kill. When you hit someone on the head, you don't necessarily intend death."

"I agree. Go on."

"It seems to me that—why are you asking *me* these questions?"

"Oh, just to see what sort of detective a mystery writer makes."

"How am I doing?"

"Great."

"It wasn't the Broadway serial killer who murdered Harry Schrumm, was it?"

"I think not."

"It was someone who wanted the police to think it was?"

He nodded. "That's a pretty safe bet."

"Which means—"

He looked directly at me. "Which means it was probably someone connected with *Knock 'Em Dead*."

He was right, of course, and I wasn't at all pleased with the conclusion. Until that moment, I'd never considered someone from the play being a suspect. Yes, there was the unbalanced Jenny Forrest who'd been fired, and Linda Amsted's alibi had been questioned. And Harry Schrumm had lots of enemies within the ranks.

But murder?

"Lieutenant Hayes, I'm afraid I'm going to need a little time to accept this new thesis."

"Sure."

"I assume you'll start again questioning everyone connected with the show."

"Detective Vasile has already started the process. But we'll be doing it casually, as though it's just routine follow-up."

"Why?"

"Because I want everyone to believe it was the serial killer who murdered Schrumm."

"Because they'll be less on their guard that way?"

"Exactly."

I fell in behind him as he left the room and rounded the corner to the stage door. Vic Righetti had been replaced by a uniformed security guard hired by Peter Monroe, the theater manager. The guard, who sat at a small table just inside the door, stood as we approached.

"Hello, Lieutenant," he said.

"Hello, Warren. This is Jessica Fletcher. She wrote the book this play is based upon."

Warren, a short, squat man with a round Irish face, smiled and shook my hand.

"Everything quiet?" Hayes asked.

"Sure."

Hayes said to me, "Everyone involved with the production has been issued an ID this morning. No one enters the theater without showing it to Warren, or to the other guard in front."

"I don't have one," I said.

"Oh, here." He handed me a laminated card from his pocket.

"Thank you."

"Buy you a cup of coffee?" Hayes asked Warren, who immediately got the hint—Hayes wanted him to leave for a few minutes. He walked away. Hayes opened the stage door to allow a cold wind to intrude.

"You said the door was open when you found Schrumm."

"That's right, although I didn't see it. I felt a breeze, which I assumed was coming through the door."

"I'm sure you were right. So Vic, the regular doorman, is asked to vacate for a few hours by a man who hands him two hundred dollars, ostensibly so that this unnamed man can meet someone without being observed. Vic goes down the street to Rafferty's, flashes his newfound wealth, and does a little drinking. During his absence, Schrumm is murdered, perhaps by whoever he was meeting."

"That scenario makes sense to me. The logical assumption is that it was Schrumm who paid Vic the money."

"But if Schrumm was killed by someone connected with the play, why would he go to such lengths to meet privately? The cast and crew routinely enter and exit the theater through the stage door. And if Schrumm didn't want anyone to know he was meeting with this anonymous person, why bother setting it up here at the Drummond? Why not meet in a hotel lobby, a restaurant, or at his apartment?"

"I don't have an answer to that."

"Neither do I. Just thinking out loud."

211

He narrowed his eyes as he said, "Here's what I want you to do, Jessica."

"I didn't realize I was supposed to do anything."

"Excuse my abruptness. Here's what I'd *like* you to do. Everyone working on *Knock 'Em Dead* knows you and I have been talking a lot. Makes sense to them, I suppose, a world-famous mystery writer getting friendly with a detective. At any rate, if you assure them that the police have absolutely no doubt that it was the Broadway serial killer who murdered Schrumm, that will accomplish what I'm after, a cast of suspects who aren't on edge whenever Vasile or I speak with them."

"I'm willing to do that. By the way, I did mention to the Factors that there might be a break in the serial murderer case."

"And?"

"They wanted to know more, of course, but since I didn't know more, I couldn't tell them."

"Good. Keep that rumor circulating with everyone."

"*Rumor*? It isn't true?"

"Let's just say it should provide comfort for them, knowing we're getting closer to nailing the serial killer. I feel good making people comfortable."

"What if the press gets wind of it?"

"They already have. The commissioner held a

press conference at two this afternoon to announce we've developed significant leads in the case."

"To make people comfortable."

"You might say that. Go on back and enjoy the rehearsal. Looks to me as though your new producer, Mrs. Factor, is whipping the troops into shape for previews and opening night."

Chapter 20

Although I had not become fond of Arnold and Jill Factor over the past six months, I had to admit that Jill seemed to be working wonders with the cast and crew of *Knock 'Em Dead*. The bickering and backbiting had ebbed, and Cyrus Walpole had the actors and actresses working together smoothly, even with the never-ending stream of rewrites from Aaron Manley's laptop computer.

Walpole called a break at four; rehearsal would resume again at four-thirty. April Larsen joined me in the darkened theater.

"Looks like it's shaping up," I said.

"It is going a little better," she said, sighing and twirling a strand of hair that had fallen over her forehead.

"Mrs. Factor seems to know what she's doing."

April looked at me as though I'd just claimed

the earth was flat. She smiled sweetly and said, "Spoken like a true Broadway neophyte."

I ignored the pettiness of the comment and said, "I was speaking with Lieutenant Hayes before. He told me the police commissioner announced at a press conference this afternoon that there's been a break in the Broadway serial killer's case."

"Bully for them," April said. "Maybe we'll find out who did mankind a service by killing Harry."

I couldn't help but grimace at the cruelty of the statement.

"That may sound callous," she added, "but then again you never really did get to know the great Harry Schrumm."

"You have pretty strong feelings about him," I said. "But I suppose all the troubles the two of you had back in Hollywood are behind them."

"You know about that?"

"I recently learned of it. All I'm trying to do is come up with reasons why you would be so negative about him to the extent of not caring that he was murdered."

"Jessica," she said, placing her fingertips on my arm and adopting the tone of a teacher about to deliver a complicated lesson, "Harry Schrumm lived his life as an unprincipled bastard. He didn't care about anything or anyone except Harry Schrumm. He stole, he lied, he destroyed careers. *That* sort of person is seldom mourned."

"But he also made careers, didn't he?"

"Hired people to appear in his shows? Yes. Made careers? Hardly."

"Yet with all the bad feelings between you and Harry, he reached out for you to star in this play, and you readily accepted."

"It's called being pragmatic. The character you created, Samantha, is a juicy one. This play, if handled properly, will be a Broadway smash and run for a very long time. I needed the work. When Harry called, my first instinct was to yell a few obscenities at him and hang up. But he can be as charming and persuasive as I can be practical and hard-nosed. He wanted me for Samantha, and I needed a decent role. It's the definition of a good deal. We both got what we were after. Excuse me. Nature calls."

As I watched her walk away, I realized that I was now looking at everyone connected with *Knock 'Em Dead* from a very different perspective. Until an hour ago, I saw the cast and crew as nothing more than creative professionals bringing my book to life on a Broadway stage. Now, after my conversation with Lieutenant Hayes, they were all suspects in the murder of Harry Schrumm. Every one of them.

Was April Larsen's hatred of Schrumm sufficient to have prompted her to kill him? That was a possibility, although it didn't make sense for her to do away with the man who handed her what she considered a juicy starring role on Broadway. Then again, it was always possible that Schrumm had thrown her some sort of a curve that sent her into a rage.

Wendell Watson had taken to sitting a few rows in back of me whenever we were at the theater and had been there when I spoke with April. He now joined me.

"She seems like a real nice lady," he said.

"Very nice," I said, not as convinced as I sounded.

"You know who I don't like?"

I was surprised there was anyone he would dislike and that he would feel free to express it.

"Who, Wendell?"

"Her." He pointed at Jill Factor.

"Why?"

"I heard her say something to one of the actresses about me."

"What did she say?"

"She said she wished that dumb hick wasn't always hanging around."

"That's not very kind."

"I sure didn't take kindly to it."

"I don't blame you, Wendell. But try to forget about it. Sheriff Metzger and the others from Cabot Cove will be here in a day. You'll enjoy yourselves and forget about comments like that."

"I'll try," he said.

"Could we please get started?" Jill Factor shouted from the stage. To Cy Walpole: "Would it be asking too much for the director to exercise some control over his cast and start directing again?"

"I gave them a break," Walpole protested weakly.

"And I've ended the break. Places everyone! We'll take it from the top."

I left my seat and went to the stage apron as the cast meandered into place. Peter Monroe, the Drummond's manager, came from the rear of the house and handed Walpole an envelope. "This was just delivered for you," he said.

"Who delivered it?" Walpole asked.

"I don't know. It was handed to the security guard at the front door."

Walpole tore open the envelope, pulled a single sheet of paper from it, brought his half-glasses down to his nose from where they'd been resting on top of his head, and scowled as he read. It was obviously a short message; it took him only a few seconds to read it. He looked out into the auditorium, his face set in anger and, I thought, concern.

"Where are the police?" he asked loudly.

"What's wrong?" I asked.

"*This* is what's wrong," he said, tossing the paper and envelope in my direction.

I picked up the envelope. Hand printed on it in block letters was WALPOLE.

I picked up the paper that had been in the envelope. The same handwritten block letters spelled out a terse, pointed communication: YOU'RE NEXT YOU TUBBY CLOWN!

"Is Lieutenant Hayes still here?" I asked aloud.

He appeared from the wings and came to me. I handed him the note.

"Who was this meant for?" he asked.

"Me," Walpole said.

I handed Hayes the envelope with Walpole's name on it.

"How did you get this?" Hayes asked.

"It was delivered to the security guard," Monroe answered.

"I'll go talk to him," Hayes said, heading up the aisle. I followed.

The guard, in response to Hayes's questions, said a man wearing a gray overcoat and black knit cap had handed it to him, saying it was important that Mr. Walpole receive it immediately.

"You get a look at his face?" Hayes asked.

The guard shrugged, licked his lips. "No, I didn't. Just a man. Just a face."

"Did he have a beard?"

"I don't think so."

"Height? Weight?"

"Average. Normal."

Hayes turned to me. "Sounds like a description of the man who bumped into you on the street and cut your coat."

I nodded.

Hayes asked the guard, "Sure it was a man? Couldn't have been a woman?"

Another shrug, a brow furrowed in thought. "Could have been. I didn't really look. I mean, all he was doing was delivering an envelope for Mr. Walpole. Why should I look at him that closely?"

"You're right," Hayes said. "Thanks."

We started to return to the auditorium when Hayes stopped, looked around, then asked me, "Are *you* sure it was a man who bumped you?"

"No," I said. "I assumed it because he—whoever it was—was dressed like a man. The coat, the hat. But yes, it could have been a woman."

Jenny Forrest? I wondered. She'd been fired by Linda Amsted, but it had been Cyrus Walpole's instructions to get rid of her. They'd been at each other's throats from the first day of rehearsals. And she had to be equally angry at Harry Schrumm. He was, after all, the producer, and it would be logical that he had to approve her firing.

I forced myself to think back to the brief encounter I'd had on the street with the man in the overcoat. Could it have been a woman? Could it have been Jenny Forrest? Would she have blamed me, too, for her dismissal from the cast?

I decided it hadn't been Jenny who'd bumped into me and cut my coat. She wasn't right physically, slighter than the person in the gray overcoat.

Then again . . .

"What do you make of the note?" Hayes asked Walpole after we'd returned to the stage where the rehearsal was at a standstill.

"The bloody Broadway serial killer," he shot back. "Why can't you find the bastard and put him away?"

Hayes said, calmly, "We're getting close, Mr. Walpole. Very close. It won't be long before the serial killer is out of business, and we'll know who killed Harry Schrumm."

"It's about time," Walpole said, sulking from the stage.

"Come back here," Jill Factor called after him. "The rehearsal."

He stopped, turned, and gave her the sort of single finger gesture usually reserved for irate drivers who've been rudely cut off.

Hayes looked at me and raised his eyebrows.

"Have time for another talk?" I asked.

"I thought you'd never ask," he said.

Chapter 21

Lieutenant Vasile was in the costume and prop room when we arrived. He was seated in a yellow canvas director's chair with his eyes closed, either napping or deep in thought.

"Tony, wake up," Hayes said.

Vasile slowly opened his eyes and smiled.

"Who was it this time?" Hayes asked. "Sharon Stone or Sandra Bullock?"

Vasile straightened up in the chair and shook his head. "I wasn't dreaming. Meg Ryan. I wasn't asleep."

"What *were* you doing?" Hayes asked nonchalantly.

"Thinking about this case."

"Schrumm?"

"And the doorman, Righetti." Vasile looked at me. "What's with you?" he asked. "You join the force?"

Hayes answered for me. "Mrs. Fletcher is our unpaid consultant on the serial killer case."

"That so?" Vasile said, adding a crooked smile. "Henry ought to give you a badge and a gun."

"I can do without both," I said. "If you'd rather I not be here, I'll—"

"No, no," Vasile said, "welcome to the team. You got it figured out yet?"

"You mean who killed Harry Schrumm? No."

Vasile asked Hayes, "Have you told her the ME's read on cause of death?"

"Yes," Hayes said, absently going through costumes on the rolling rack. A crude sign taped to it said ACT ONE.

"So, Ms. Unpaid Consultant, what does that say to you?" Vasile asked.

I didn't hesitate: "It says to me that it wasn't the serial killer who murdered him. It was someone who wanted us to *think* it was another serial killer victim."

"Hey, she's good, Henry," Vasile said to his partner, laughing.

"May I offer another observation?" I asked.

"Please do," Hayes said.

"If Harry Schrumm was killed by a blow to his left temple, it means the blow was delivered by a right-handed person."

"Maybe she's not so good," Vasile said. "It

could have been a left-handed person hitting him from behind."

"I don't think so," I said. "As Lieutenant Hayes and I have discussed, hitting someone in the head isn't usually a premeditated act. Of course, it can be, but I don't believe that was the case with Harry Schrumm. If I were painting the picture of how he died, I'd say he was in an argument that got out of hand—and was facing his assailant."

"An argument with who?" Vasile asked.

"I don't have an answer for that, Detective, but I think the list can be narrowed down."

"We're listening," Hayes said.

I thought for a moment before continuing. "Harry Schrumm, as you know, was a short man, no taller than five feet, five inches."

"Five four and a half," Hayes said. "The ME measured the corpse."

"All right, five feet, four and a half inches," I said. "He was struck on his left temple. Did the medical examiner indicate whether he was struck squarely, or was it a glancing blow, meaning had it come from above or below?"

"Straight on," Vasile answered. "Blunt force injury to the weakest part of the head, the temple. Fighters go down when an opponent catches them just right on that particular spot."

"Which means," I said, "that Schrumm was hit

in the temple by someone not much taller than he was."

Hayes and Vasile looked at each other and smiled, which made me feel good enough to proceed with my thesis.

"If that's true—and it's only supposition on my part—it means you can rule out members of the cast and crew who are considerably taller than Harry Schrumm."

"Fair enough," Vasile said. "We'll line everybody up and mark their height on the wall, like my mother did with me and my five brothers."

"Must have been quite a family," I said, laughing. "But I don't think it's necessary to go to that length. It's fairly obvious just by looking at the people involved with *Knock 'Em Dead* who's tall, and who's short."

"Any of the women in the show qualify," Hayes said.

"Except April Larsen," I said. "She's a tall woman."

"Not *that* tall," Vasile said.

"No, not that tall," I repeated because he was right. Although she was five feet, seven inches tall, that wouldn't automatically preclude her from the suspect list.

The tallest person, aside from some male crew members—I decided to remove all crew members from my suspect list, at least for the time being, because I wasn't aware that any of them had had a rancorous relationship with Schrumm—was the director, Cy Walpole.

Did that mean he was ruled out in my mind as a possible suspect? Only if my scenario about height determining possible guilt was valid. As much as it made sense to me, I'd been around enough murder investigations not to dismiss anyone as a suspect based upon conjecture. Walpole's relationship with Harry Schrumm wasn't especially combative, but it wasn't friendly either.

Aaron Manley fit the height requirement. He looked taller than he was because of his slender build and the way he carried himself. There had been no love lost between the producer and the playwright.

The second tallest cast member was Brett Burton, the brooding hulk who played Jerry, the oldest son in the play. The problem with considering him a viable suspect was that I had no idea what his relationship with Harry Schrumm had been. He certainly had the physique to deliver a lethal blow to anyone's temple.

There was, of course, Linda Amsted. She was the right height. She was rumored to be one of Schrumm's girlfriends. And she'd been placed in a position of authority by Schrumm.

Too, another rumor had her romantically, or simply sexually, involved with Brett Burton. Did this create in Harry Schrumm a level of jealousy that could have erupted into a confrontation between the two men? Not if my deduction about height being a determining factor held water.

David Potts, who played the younger son, was short, too. In terms of feet and inches, he was a possibility. But like Brett Burton, I knew nothing of his relationship with Schrumm.

And then there were the Factors. Plenty of tension between them and Harry Schrumm over money. They'd invested heavily in *Knock 'Em Dead*, and certainly weren't brimming with confidence over Schrumm's way of doing business. Arnold Factor was too tall; his wife, Jill, was just the right height to have delivered the killing blow to Harry's head.

Hayes said to his partner, "I've asked Mrs. Fletcher to keep spreading the rumor among the cast and crew that we're certain the serial killer murdered Schrumm, and that we're close to a break."

"But do you *really* have leads in that case?" I asked.

"We're getting there," Vasile said.

"That's good to hear," I said. "I think I'll go out and watch some more of the rehearsal. Previews are right around the corner."

"Besides, your bodyguard is probably getting

nervous," Vasile said. "Is this guy really a security guard where you come from?"

"That's right," I said. "Our sheriff recommended him. You'll meet Sheriff Metzger. He's coming to New York with a group from Cabot Cove."

"I can't wait," Vasile said.

I gave him a disapproving look and went to open the door.

"One thing," Hayes said.

"What's that?"

"If Schrumm was murdered by someone in the cast or crew, that same person is right here in this theater. If he or she thinks you're a little too effective in your snooping, Jessica, you could be in jeopardy. In other words, watch your back."

"Thanks for the concern," I said, opening the door and standing face to face with Linda Amsted, who'd obviously been out there during our conversation.

"Hello," I said. "Back from Hollywood?"

"Just got in."

"Can I do something for you, Ms. Amsted?" Hayes asked.

"No," she said. "I was just—I was on my way out the stage door."

"Uh-huh," Hayes said. "I'd like some time with you if you don't mind."

"I'm late for an appointment."

"With Roy Richardson again?" Hayes asked.

"As a matter of fact, yes."

"I sat in on one of his classes this morning," I said.

"So I heard," she replied. "Well, excuse me. As I said, I'm running late."

"Are you coming back here?" Hayes asked.

"I hadn't planned on it."

"Why don't you change your plans, Ms. Amsted," Vasile said, his tone hard, the message unmistakable.

She glared at him. "All right. I will change my plans."

I closed the door behind us and followed her around the corner to the stage door, where the guard sat reading a magazine.

"Are you all right?" I asked.

"Yes. Actually, no."

"Care to share it with me?"

She glanced at the guard, who seemed disinterested in our conversation.

"I've been threatened," she whispered to me.

"Threatened?" I said in an equally low voice. "By whom?"

"I don't know. I received a note at my office."

"Cy received a threatening note at the theater a little while ago," I said.

"He did? What did it say?"

"It said 'You're next,' along with a few unflattering descriptive words."

"Mine said the same thing," Linda said.

"Do you have it with you?"

"No. I left it at the office."

"You should give it to the police, to Lieutenant Hayes or his partner."

She guffawed and spoke louder. "No thanks. The less I get involved with them the better."

"But—"

"I have to go, Jessica. I'll be back later."

A cold wind swept through the stage door as she departed. It closed with a dense metallic clang.

"They're predicting snow tonight," the guard said, looking up from his magazine.

"It's that time of year," I said, walking away, passing the closed door to the prop and costume room where the two detectives were huddled, along the hallway, through the darkened section— I made a mental note to ask Peter Monroe to replace the bulbs—and to the wings from where I could watch the rehearsal that was underway. I'd been there only a minute when a scream filled the entire theater, reverberating from every wall, filling every crevice and eardrum. Then, deathly silence, followed by the sound of running feet from the opposite backstage area. All heads turned to see Pamela South rush from the wings to the middle of the stage.

"What the hell is going on?" Jill Factor demanded in a loud voice from where she sat in the front row of the empty house.

Pamela stood center stage, shaking, crying, her arms wrapped tightly about herself.

"What happened?" Cy Walpole asked.

"I saw him," Pamela gasped.

"Saw who?" Charles Flowers said as he came to Pamela and placed his hands on her shoulders.

"The ghost," she managed. "Marcus Drummond."

Chapter 22

Pamela South's "sighting" of the ghost of Marcus Drummond created instant chaos onstage. Some laughed. "Was he giving acting lessons?" someone quipped. Others tried to comfort Pamela, who'd sunk to her knees and was crying uncontrollably. Aaron Manley, obviously disgusted, left the stage, announcing he needed a drink. Jill Factor tried to exhibit patience but eventually ran out of it and demanded that the rehearsal resume.

Pamela got to her feet, came to the apron and said to Jill, like a performer delivering a soliloquy to the audience, "I'm out of here. First Harry, then the doorman, now the ghost of Marcus Drummond decides to show up. Good-bye!"

"Wait a minute," Walpole said. "You can't walk out now. Why don't you get yourself a drink or something to calm down?"

"I'm history with this damn play," Pamela said. "Nothing's worth losing my life."

"You can't do this!" Jill shouted. "Previews are two days away. You don't have an understudy."

"Shove your previews," Pamela said. "This show is jinxed, spooked, doomed. See you around." With that she bounded down the stairs to the auditorium and ran up the aisle toward the lobby.

Detectives Hayes and Vasile, who'd left the theater to get something to eat, now joined the chaos.

"What happened?" Vasile asked. "What the hell is going on?"

"A ghost," Walpole said disgustedly. "One of the cast met Marcus Drummond."

Hayes laughed. "I've been dying to meet him myself."

"I can't believe this," Jill said, slapping her hands against her thighs and pacing in front of the stage.

"She's frightened, poor thing," I said.

Jill spun around and fixed me in a hateful stare. "She's frightened? Isn't that sweet? She's frightened, and Arnie and I are facing bankruptcy if this show doesn't open as scheduled."

"Maybe I can talk to her," I offered. "I thought I saw the ghost, too, and—"

Jill walked away to where the cast had gathered stage left. As she did, Arnold came down the aisle, stopped, looked around, and asked, "What did I do, walk into a wake by mistake? I thought—"

"Oh, shut up," Jill said.

Arnold came over to me, hands outstretched in a plea for an explanation.

I explained the circumstances leading to Pamela South's quitting the show.

"Now? At this late date?"

"I'm afraid so."

Jill joined us. "We'd better talk," she told her husband.

"I'd say so," he said. They walked up the aisle together, presumably to find a quiet place to explore their alternatives.

I went over to where Wendell Watson sat alone in the center of the house.

"I suppose this sort of thing happens in the theater," I said in reaction to his worried expression.

"She saw a ghost?" he said, voice quivering.

I laughed. "Of course she didn't see a ghost, Wendell. She *thought* she saw a ghost. It's a silly legend about this theater."

"But I believe in ghosts, Mrs. Fletcher."

I sat next to him. "You do?"

He nodded. "My uncle Jimmy lived in a haunted house in Cabot Cove. He had to sell it because they kept him and his wife awake every night."

"Oh."

I was spared having to explain my lack of belief in ghosts when Linda Amsted suddenly appeared on stage.

"You'd better find the Factors," Walpole told her. "Pamela has quit the show."

"*What?*"

"You heard me. Find the Factors and come up with a replacement."

"You're joking."

"No, he's not joking," Joe McCartney said.

"Where did they go?" Linda asked.

"That way," Walpole said, pointing.

"We want to talk to you," Vasile said to Linda.

"I know, I know, but this is more important." She headed in the direction taken by the Factors.

Vasile started after her, but Hayes grabbed his arm and shook his head. I lip-read, "Later."

I sat with Wendell while the cast and crew wandered about the theater, not knowing what to do, or what was in store for them as far as the play was concerned. I shared their confusion. Did this mean, at best, a postponement of the previews and opening of *Knock 'Em Dead*?

That prospect was not pleasant.

It was a half hour later when the Factors and Linda Amsted reappeared.

Jill said, "All right, everyone, here's what's happening. We've replaced Pamela in the show."

We all looked at each other. Who could possibly

step in at such a late moment to fill an important role? Who could learn all those lines in little more than a day?

"Who's replacing her?" Walpole asked.

"Jenny Forrest," Jill answered.

Chapter 23

The rehearsal resumed after a half hour of responses to the news that Jenny Forrest, the original Marcia in *Knock 'Em Dead*, would be rejoining the cast. Reactions were mixed. Cyrus Walpole let out a string of obscenities in his charming British accent; David Potts, playing the younger son with a romantic interest in Marcia, was delighted with the news: "She's the best actress I've ever worked with." April Larsen said she felt faint and slouched in a chair; a stagehand brought her a glass of water and a wet towel.

My reaction was to become numb.

Lieutenant Hayes came to where I sat with Wendell.

"There's no business like show business," he said, smiling.

"I'm not so sure it's a business," I said.

"How are you going to feel about being around the erratic Ms. Forrest?" he asked.

"I'll manage," I said, "provided she doesn't decide to attack me again."

"Who attacked you?" Wendell asked.

"The actress who is going to replace the one who quit."

"The one Sheriff Metzger told me about? That's why he sent me to New York as your bodyguard."

"I know, but it's nothing for you to be concerned about, Wendell. It wasn't a *real* attack. It wasn't a *real* knife."

"When is she due here?" Hayes asked.

"I heard the Factors say they'd reached her by phone and that she'd be at the theater within the hour."

The security guard at the front door came to the auditorium and called for Hayes. A minute later, the detective returned, followed by Jenny Forrest. She'd been denied access to the Drummond because she didn't have one of the passes issued by the NYPD, but Hayes had cleared her.

She walked with confidence, head high, down the aisle, went directly to the stage, came up to Cy Walpole and said, a smile on her face, hands on her hips, "Here I am, Mr. Director. Ready?"

Walpole's face turned beet red, and I silently prayed he wouldn't have a stroke. Jill broke the tension by saying, "All right, we have our original

Marcia back. I suggest we forget everything that's gone before and get down to the business of whipping this play into opening night shape. Places!"

I returned to my suite at the Westin Central Park South a little after midnight. The rehearsal had gone well with Jenny Forrest back in the cast as Marcia. Walpole and the others obviously recognized that there was a lot more at stake than their personal feelings about Jenny and dug into their parts with renewed vigor. Aaron Manley, who appeared to me to have had more than a single drink, tried to inject some rewrites, but Jill brought him up short. "The script we have is the script we'll go with," she said sternly. "There's been enough tampering with it to last a lifetime."

"I bloody well agree," Walpole said.

And so they rehearsed into the night. Jenny never acknowledged me and I was grateful for that. I wasn't sure how I would react if she approached me and was content to keep my distance. One thing was certain: She made a much better Marcia than Pamela South had, and Dave Potts's performance was elevated a few notches in his scenes with her.

Detectives Hayes and Vasile had left the theater at ten. On their way out, Hayes stopped to tell me that he intended to have plainclothes detectives in the audience for the previews—"Just in case the serial killer views it as a dramatic moment to strike again." His parting words, whispered in my ear, were, "Remember what I said about watching your back, Jessica."

I was happy to return to the hotel. I changed into my pajamas, put on a fluffy terrycloth robe provided by the Westin, ordered smoked salmon and sparkling water from room service, and perused the pile of phone messages handed me at the desk when I arrived. It was too late to return most of them, but I knew my agent would be up; Matt's message was to call any time up until two.

"How's things?" he asked.

Going through the litany of events was too exhausting to contemplate, so I simply said, "Fine. How was your trip?" He'd been in Los Angeles negotiating film deals for other clients.

"Great. Everything went smoothly. I read that the Factors are now producing *Knock 'Em Dead*."

"That's right."

"I'll have to call them in the morning. There was a payment to you due one week prior to previews. I haven't seen any check."

"They've been so busy picking up the pieces after Harry Schrumm's murder, I don't doubt they've let administrative matters slip."

"Nice of you to make excuses for them, Jess, but a deal's a deal. There's another payment due the day of opening night. I don't want them to fall too far behind."

"I'm ready for bed," I said. "Can we touch base tomorrow?"

"Count on it. Will you be at the theater?"

"Not for most of the day. My friends from Cabot Cove are arriving at about noon. I want to be here to greet them and get them settled. But we'll be at dress rehearsal. That starts at four."

"I'll swing by after four," he said. "Excited about the opening night of previews?"

"I haven't really had time to get excited, but now that you mention it, yes, I am very excited. You'll be there?"

"Of course. Schrumm's office provided Susan and me tickets. We're sitting with Vaughan and Olga Buckley."

"Should be quite a night."

"Should be." He chuckled. "I was going to say 'break a leg,' but considering everything that's happened, maybe I shouldn't."

"Your discretion is appreciated. See you tomorrow."

The conversation with Matt left me wide awake. In all the commotion since dinner last September in New York when Matt announced that *Knock 'Em Dead* had been optioned for Broadway, the true impact had gotten lost for me. The ensuing months had become a blur of personal conflicts, runaway egos, things going wrong, and, of course, murder. But now, as I stood by the window and looked out over the imposing concrete canyons and neon splendor of Manhattan, the reality of the play opening to live audiences hit home. It was a delicious expectation, and I couldn't contain an involuntary giggle.

Knock 'Em Dead would open on time. The previews were sold-out; so were the first ten months of regular nightly performances. That morning's *New York Times* had carried a two-page ad for the play in which my name was larger than anyone else's from the show. Stories had been appearing in every publication about the play, sadly fueled to a great extent by the tragedies surrounding the Drummond Theater, and Broadway in general. I'd felt somewhat guilty about not cooperating with Priscilla Hoye's requests for me to make myself available for radio and television interviews, but I simply couldn't bring myself to do them. She'd been gracious about my constant refusals and had managed to mount an impressive publicity campaign without me. Maybe now that the play was about to be an actuality, I'd feel differently, especially if the reviews were kind.

I climbed into bed thinking about the arrival of my dear friends from Cabot Cove. All arrangements had been made for them to attend the dress rehearsal and opening night of previews. It would be wonderful being surrounded by their warmth and unabashed enthusiasm for me and the play.

I fell asleep humming, badly, "Another Opening, Another Show."

The worst was over, the best was yet to come. *Wasn't it?*

Chapter 24

"This is so exciting," Pat Hitchcock, Cabot Cove's most popular nurse and our town's "Woman of the Year," said when I met my hometown contingent in the hotel lobby a little past noon. "We're actually going to the dress rehearsal?"

"Yes," I said, "and opening night of previews. But remember, things might be a little rough, some bumps to be smoothed out before opening night."

"Will all the critics and celebrities be there?" Mort Metzger's wife asked.

"I have no idea whether they review Broadway plays during previews or on opening night," I said. "I'm new to this."

Everyone laughed.

"How was your acting lesson, Jessica?" Seth Hazlitt asked.

"My what? Oh, yes, my acting lesson. It was—interesting."

Wendell stood behind me.

"Have you been behavin' yourself?" Sheriff Metzger asked him. Seeing Mort in civilian clothes was always a shock to me. He seemed to live in his uniform in Cabot Cove.

Wendell grinned sheepishly at him. "Sure have, Sheriff."

"He's been a wonderful bodyguard," I said. "The best."

"Good to hear. Now, what about this serial killer who's been running around loose on Broadway? They still haven't nailed him?"

"I'm afraid not," I said, "but let's not talk about him. We're here to celebrate *Knock 'Em Dead*, not real murder. Is everyone hungry? I've reserved a table for us at the Redeye Grill." I shielded my mouth with my hand to feign passing along a very important and secret point: "It's a v-e-r-y 'in' place. We're only going to 'in' places."

"Oooh," said Beth Mullin, owner with her husband, Peter, of Cabot Cove's flower shop. "Did everyone hear that? We're only going to the 'in' places."

"Come on," I said. "It's a popular restaurant. We don't want to be late and lose the table."

After a wonderful lunch punctuated by effervescent conversation, we walked to the Drummond

Theater on West Forty-fourth Street, where the guard perused a list of names I'd provided Lieutenant Hayes, checking each of my friends off as they entered.

We paused in the lobby. "Just a word of caution," I told them. "These are temperamental people, and a dress rehearsal is bound to be tense. All I'm saying is that we have to be quiet. You know, sort of fade into the background. Harry Schrumm, the original producer who was killed, arranged for you to be here. The new producers, Mr. and Mrs. Factor, were reluctant to honor my request for you to be at the dress rehearsal. So, let's just stay out of their way. Okay?"

"Fine by me," Seth said. "Wouldn't want to offend anybody's artistic temperament." His pique was evident.

We entered the auditorium.

"We'll sit there," I said, indicating the center section, toward the rear. Technicians were busy preparing the stage for Act One. Jill and Arnold Factor huddled with Cyrus Walpole at stage right. The cast, I assumed, was backstage having makeup applied and changing into opening act costumes.

I looked for Detectives Hayes and Vasile but didn't see them. Nor were there any uniformed officers, with the exception of the private security guard at the front entrance, and undoubtedly the one positioned at the stage door.

My friends seemed enthralled with what was going on in the theater. So was I. This was the first time I'd get to see *Knock 'Em Dead* in its entirety, straight through from beginning to end without scenes being performed out of sequence, or with the constant interruptions that had characterized earlier rehearsals.

Cy Walpole came to where a small table and microphone had been set up in the third row center. I'd been told by one of the technical crew that the director would be able to talk from that position with the lighting and sound technicians, as well as having the capability of stopping the rehearsal and giving instructions over the theater's speaker system. Hopefully, he wouldn't need to exercise that option.

Jill took the stage.

"We're about to begin," she said. "It's unusual to have anyone in the audience for a dress rehearsal, but Mrs. Fletcher was promised this courtesy and we have no choice but to go along with it."

I stiffened. Her snide comment was uncalled for.

"What does she think we are, a bunch of school kids?" Seth muttered under his breath.

Jill looked at Walpole, who'd slid behind his

makeshift third row desk. "Are we ready?" she asked.

"Yes, we're ready," he said.

"Good. Act One."

Jill joined her husband next to Walpole. The lights in the theater dimmed, in itself a dramatic moment. Then, the curtain opened to reveal the living room of my fictitious family's modest home. April Larsen and Joe McCartney, the mother and father, sat in matching easy chairs. He read a newspaper, she concentrated on needlepoint. Their reverie was interrupted by the arrival of the younger son, Joshua, played by David Potts, and his girlfriend, Marcia, her role once again in the hands of Jenny Forrest.

"Isn't that the one who attacked you?" Mort Metzger whispered to me.

"Sssh," I said, putting my finger to my lips.

The first act progressed smoothly. I was beguiled by what I saw and heard. Although Aaron Manley had rewritten much of the script, what was being spoken by the actors was very much my work. The characters and scenes I'd created were being played before my eyes. More important, others were being exposed to it simultaneously. I glanced at my friends' faces. Smiles erupted at the right times, as did frowns of concern at what was being presented between the characters.

Cy Walpole was evidently pleased because he never stopped the play to suggest changes. Even the lighting and sound cues worked to perfection, something I was led to believe seldom happened at dress rehearsals.

We were nearing the end of Act One. I'd learned from working with Manley that it was important to end each of the first two acts with a dramatic flourish. I always tried to do that with the end of each chapter of my books, but it was obviously even more crucial with a play. Act One would end with April Larsen discovering the body of her husband offstage. Her loud and pro-longed scream would bring down the curtain.

I waited with anticipation for that moment to occur, my eyes moving between the stage and my friends' faces. The entire fictitious family, now gathered on stage, were in the midst of an intense confrontation between the father and his two sons. Jerry, the oldest, flings a nasty accusation in his father's face, causing the father to storm from the room. The others leave; April Larsen sits alone, despairing over the rift that has developed within her family.

She calls out for her husband, but receives no reply. Then, she leaves the stage to look for him in their bedroom.

Now! I thought. The scream.

Maureen Metzger, who sat next to me, flinched

at the first pained hint of the howl as it arose from offstage, and grasped her husband's arm. The scream increased in intensity, filling the theater and threatening to peel the paint from its walls.

Except—the scream hadn't come from April Larsen. It took me a split second to become aware of this and then to realize it had emanated from the opposite side of the stage from where April had made her exit—the side on which the offices, dressing rooms, and costume and prop room were located—the side where Harry Schrumm had been murdered.

I stood. April ran on to the stage in response to the scream. Cy Walpole said into his microphone, "What in bloody hell is going on?"

The stage filled with cast and crew. The house lights came up. It was chaos. My friends from Cabot Cove looked at each other in shock: "What's happened?" "Is this part of the play, Jess?"

Suddenly, Charles Flowers ran to the stage from the direction of the scream: "It's the serial killer. He's got Jenny."

I immediately headed down the aisle, followed by Wendell Watson and Mort Metzger. We climbed the few steps up to the stage, went into the wings, and ran down the long hallway to where Detectives Hayes and Vasile were pressed against the wall on opposite sides of the women's dressing room door.

"The serial killer is here?" I asked, breathlessly.

"In there," Hayes said, pointing to the closed door. He motioned for us to move past them and out of the way, and we followed his silent instructions. Cold air came from around the corner, just as it had the day I discovered Harry Schrumm's body. I moved in that direction, Wendell at my side. The stage door was wide open. The security guard who'd been posted there lay on his back, a magazine at his side. Wendell immediately knelt over him and said, "Hey, you okay?"

To my relief, the guard raised his head, then slowly came up to a sitting position with Wendell's help.

Thank God, I thought. He was alive.

I moved back to where Hayes and Vasile, guns drawn, continued their vigil, whispering instructions to each other. Mort Metzger had taken a position against the wall, next to Vasile.

"One more time," Hayes said aloud to the door and whoever was behind it. "Let the girl come out. Don't hurt her. Let her go, and you come out with your hands raised."

There was no response.

I looked past the detectives to where a dozen people were congregated at the other end of the hallway. A few started in our direction, but I held up my hand. The last thing Hayes and Vasile needed was a crowd. "Are you sure Jenny is in there with him?" I asked Hayes.

"Yeah," he replied, sotto voice. "He came through the stage door, grabbed her, and shoved her in there. I happened to be coming out of one of the offices as it was happening."

"I didn't know you were in the theater," I said.

He held up his hand to silence me.

"Listen to me," he said loudly to the door, "don't be a fool. You can't go anywhere. You're going to have to come out eventually, so do it now before anybody gets hurt."

We waited; it seemed like minutes although only a few seconds elapsed before we saw the doorknob turn, and the door opened slowly. Hayes and Vasile kept their guns trained on the person standing in the doorway. It was Jenny Forrest. She had a crooked smile on her face and held her head at a defiant angle.

"Thank God you're all right," I said.

Hayes motioned for her to come fully into the hallway. She complied. We all peered into the dressing room, but saw no one.

"He's in there?" Vasile asked Jenny.

She nodded.

"Go on, get out of here," Hayes told her.

I watched Jenny deliberately leave us, but instead of walking in the direction of the onlookers at the other end of the corridor, she headed for the stage door.

I returned my attention to the room she'd just exited. Detectives Hayes and Vasile moved closer to the doorway in order to have a wider view of the room.

"Jesus," Hayes muttered, lowering his weapon and stepping inside, followed by Vasile. I took a few steps into the room and saw what had prompted his exasperated comment. Sprawled on a small couch was Roy Richardson. Blood oozed from around a knife stuck firmly into his chest.

"Get her!" Hayes commanded, spinning around and returning to the hall. *"Get her!"*

We reached the stage door in time to see Jenny Forrest's back as she left the theater and entered the alley separating it from the Von Feurston.

Wendell, who'd helped the security guard into his wooden chair, didn't hesitate. His long, lanky frame was out the door in a flash. We poured through the door and saw my young bodyguard from Cabot Cove tackle Jenny Forrest from behind, sending both of them tumbling on to the sidewalk, knocking down pedestrians, and ending up in Forty-fourth Street's gutter. Hayes and Vasile picked her up, brought her hands behind her, and cuffed her wrists. Simultaneously, marked police cars roared to a stop in front of the theater, lights blazing, a swarm of uniformed police spilling from them.

"Let's get back inside," I said to Mort and Wendell, whose green uniform was torn at the knees from hitting the pavement. We paused to see Jenny being placed in the back seat of a patrol car, then returned to the auditorium where everyone had gathered. My friends from Cabot Cove, who had been standing together at one end of the stage apron, flocked to me, as did most of the cast and crew.

"What happened?" they asked, almost as a chorus.

"I'm afraid—I'm afraid that Jenny has been arrested."

"For what?"

"For murdering someone most of you know, Roy Richardson."

"Roy?" Hanna Shawn cried out.

"Jenny killed him?" Brett Burton mumbled.

"Looks like you won't have to worry about your Broadway serial killer any more," Mort announced proudly.

"What happened to you?" someone asked Wendell, noticing his torn uniform and dirt on his face.

"This young man apprehended the murderer," Mort said. "He's a genuine hero."

"Jenny is the serial killer?" Joe McCartney said in a voice swelled with disbelief.

"Is it true?" Arnold Factor asked.

"I don't know," I said, "but it looks that way."

Lieutenants Hayes and Vasile joined us. So did Jill Factor, who'd stayed with Cy Walpole at the director's third-row desk.

"The entire Broadway theater community, and all of New York City, owes you a huge debt of gratitude," she said to the detectives in a sweet, sincere voice I'd not heard from her before.

Cy Walpole came forward. "It doesn't surprise me in the least that our Ms. Forrest turns out to be a cold-blooded killer," he said. "The question is, what do we do now for the role of Marcia?"

"Maybe our beloved casting director has the answer," Jill said, looking past us to Linda Amsted, who seemed to have suddenly, and simply, appeared from the rear of the house.

"I just arrived," she said, "and saw all the commotion out front."

I explained what had happened.

Linda slumped in an aisle seat. "Jenny Forrest a murderer," she said into the air, "and Roy Richardson a victim. That's a switch."

"But what do we do about Jenny's role?" Walpole asked.

"Get Pamela South back," Linda said matter-of-factly. "Now that the serial killer has been apprehended, she shouldn't be afraid any longer."

"There's the ghost she saw," David Potts said.

"We'll hire ghostbusters," Linda quipped, standing and walking away in search of a phone. She returned twenty minutes later to announce that Pamela South was on her way to the theater.

The rehearsal resumed an hour later. I sat with my Cabot Cove friends and watched the cast once again attempt to get through the play without interruption. Although the energy level was down, particularly Dave Potts, who wasn't as comfortable playing his scenes with Pamela as he'd been with Jenny, and despite the heavy, palpable air of murder that hung over the theater—the backstage area, especially the dressing rooms, were declared off-limits, necessitating the removal of all the costumes to the small offices that lined the hallway—and the loss of concentration created by the night's nontheatrical events, it went well, as well as could be expected. My friends applauded loudly when the final curtain came down and the house lights came up.

I looked across the theater and was surprised to see Lieutenant Hayes sitting alone.

"I thought you'd left," I said.

"I intended to, but decided to see whether your play would come together after everything that's happened. Looks like it has."

"I think so."

"You were lucky to have that other actress ready to step in."

"I agree, although I'm not sure she makes as good a Marcia as Jenny Forrest."

"Maybe not, but she's a lot less lethal. By the way, Ms. Forrest *is* the Broadway serial killer. Tony Vasile says she hasn't stopped babbling about it since she arrived at headquarters. She's certifiably insane. Well, I've got to be going. Tony's at the precinct helping start the arraignment process. I'd better get back to help him. He gets his Italian dander up if he thinks I'm not pulling my weight."

The amplified voice of Cyrus Walpole filled the theater. "We'll take a half hour break, then gather for my comments and notes. I know it's late, but we still have some adjusting to do before previews tomorrow night."

"Are you staying for the postmortem?" Hayes asked me.

"Yes, and I wish you would, too."

His eyebrows went up. "Why?"

"Something that occurred to me while I was watching the end of the third act."

"Maybe you should tell your director."

"Oh, I will. But I'd feel better if you were present. Please?"

"All right. I'll call Tony and tell him I'm running late."

I spent the next half hour with my friends. Naturally, the real murderous events took conversational priority over *Knock 'Em Dead*, although there was plenty of talk about it, too.

"Sure you want to stay to hear what the director has to say?" I asked them. "You'll see the results tomorrow night—without anyone getting killed as an unplanned intermission. It's late. You must be exhausted."

"We wouldn't miss a minute of it, Jess," Peter Eder said. "The play would make a great musical. Maybe you can mention that to your producers."

"I'll introduce you," I said. "Excuse me." I went to where Linda Amsted sat alone, obviously very much into her private thoughts.

"Mind an intrusion?" I asked.

"What? Oh, sure, Jess. I was just thinking."

"About what?" I asked, sitting next to her.

"I was thinking about Roy."

"I only met him that once at his acting class," I said, "and must admit I didn't especially like him. But when you're dead, all those bets are off, as they say. Tragic."

"He knew about Jenny."

Her statement stunned me into momentary silence.

"Shocked, Jess? I was too when he told me. He wasn't certain, of course, but he was convinced she was the serial killer. Roy was very much in love with her."

"I didn't know that."

"And he thought she was the best young actress he'd ever coached. Of course, they were both a bit mad. The only difference was that Roy was content to take out his madness on his students through verbal abuse and character assassination. Jenny needed greater satisfaction."

"He told me he hoped the serial killer turned out to be one of his acting students," I said. "He was obviously toying with me."

"Roy toyed with everyone."

"Do you know why he came here tonight?"

She shook her head. "Unless he was going to make his final attempt at getting her to stop running around killing people. He succeeded, didn't he?"

"And he paid for it with his life. So did Harry Schrumm."

"Yes, poor, poor Harry. I shall miss him. I'll miss everyone."

"All right everybody, gather round for Uncle Cy's critique," Walpole announced through the speakers.

"Coming?" I asked, standing.

"No. I'm going home. Maybe we'll touch base before you go back to Maine." She stood, too, and took my hand. "I hope *Knock 'Em Dead* is a smash, Jess. I really do. Take care. You're a terrific woman."

Tears formed in my eyes as I watched her go

up the aisle and disappear into the lobby. 'I'll miss everyone,' she'd said. Was she suicidal? Had she lost too many people in her life to want to go on living? All I could do was hope that wasn't the case, and I silently pledged to call her first thing in the morning.

Cy Walpole's notes about the performance were long and detailed. For the most part, they were complimentary to the cast and crew.

When he was through, Jill and Arnold Factor stood and delivered what was intended to be a pep talk. They spoke for ten minutes, heaping praise on everyone connected with the show. Jill ended with, "Unfortunately we've all been forced to confront real murder instead of just make-believe. If there is such a thing as closure, we can thank this wonderful detective and all his people for solving the mystery of who killed Harry Schrumm, and all the others who suffered at the hands of the Broadway serial killer. It makes me shudder to think that someone as close to us as Jenny has turned out to be a vicious killer."

"Well, it's been a long night," Arnold said. "I wish a broken leg for everyone tomorrow night. The celebration party is on us."

He and Jill beamed at each other.

I stood.

"Oh, yes, I almost forgot," Jill said. "None of us would be here if it wasn't for the fertile and creative mind of Jessica Fletcher. We're all in your debt, Jessica."

The Factors applauded. Others joined in. When they were finished, I said, "I think before we call it a night, I'd like to thank everyone for being so gracious to me on this, my baptism on Broadway. You've all been very kind."

"Our pleasure," Aaron Manley said, standing and stretching. "God, I'm tired."

Others began gathering their things.

"Mrs. Factor," I said.

She'd been walking away arm-in-arm with her husband. She turned.

"Yes?"

"Was it money that caused you and Arnold to kill Harry Schrumm?"

Lieutenant Hayes, who'd been sitting next to me, stood.

"Would you repeat that?" Jill said.

"I asked whether it was a disagreement over money that led to you killing Harry Schrumm."

Jill closed the distance between us. "Are you crazy?"

"I don't think so."

"Harry Schrumm was killed by that insane young woman, Jenny Forrest."

"No," I said, "Jenny didn't kill him."

"Come on," Arnold said to his wife, grabbing her arm. "Let's get out of here."

Hayes stepped in their path and said pleasantly, "I'd like to hear more of this."

Arnold started to say something but Jill snapped, "Shut up. Go on, Mrs. Fletcher. I think your too-active writer's imagination is working overtime."

"How did you know that the pipe wedged in Harry's mouth was the one used as a prop in the play?"

"I—I read about it."

"No, you didn't. None of the press accounts of the murder reported that. But Arnold mentioned it when I was at your apartment."

"I did?" he asked.

"Yes, you did. You're desperate for money, aren't you? Otherwise, you wouldn't have offered to sell me half your share in the play at a discounted price."

"I find this quite offensive, Mrs. Fletcher, and don't feel compelled to respond to anything you say. But for your information, I learned about the pipe from Joe." She nodded at Joe McCartney, who smoked a pipe during the performance.

McCartney said, "I never told you about the pipe. Why would I? There were three or four pipes in the prop room and I just grabbed another one. I never said a word to you or anyone else about it."

I said, "You didn't mean to kill him, I'm sure.

But it must have been a very intense argument to cause you to hit him in the head. When you saw he was dead from the blow, you stabbed him in the chest and arranged the hat and pipe on him to make it appear like another serial killing." I turned to her husband. "Or was it you, Arnold, who did the stabbing of a dead man? It's too unladylike an act for your wife to commit."

Arnold stepped forward, hands outstretched. "Look," he said, "this is getting out of hand. You don't understand the pressure we've been under. It wasn't my idea. I—"

Jill was carrying a heavy flashlight she used to read from the script in the darkened theater. She swung it at her husband, catching him on the left temple. He fell to one knee, his hand touching the blood that ran down on to his glistening, starched white tux shirt and the shoulder of his black tuxedo jacket.

"You could have been a contender, Mrs. Factor," Lieutenant Hayes said. "In a boxing ring, not on Broadway."

"Good night," Jill said, marching up the aisle, leaving her dazed husband behind. Hayes helped him to his feet.

"Mrs. Fletcher makes sense," the detective said.

"I didn't kill Harry," Arnold said.

"But you did kill Vic, the doorman, didn't you?" I said. "It was you who gave him the bribe to vacate his post so that you and Jill could meet secretly with Harry. I imagine Jill realized that Vic might identify you as having bribed him to leave the stage door. He had to be killed, too."

"Am I free to go?" Arnold asked Hayes, pressing a handkerchief to his bleeding temple.

"You're free to go with me to headquarters to answer some questions," Hayes said. "Don't worry about ordering a limo for your wife. A police cruiser will do just fine."

Arnold didn't offer any resistance when Hayes took him by the arm and started to lead him from the theater. The detective said to me as he passed, "Any time you'd like to change careers, Mrs. Fletcher, and run down real murderers, give me a call."

I smiled. "Thanks, but no thanks, Lieutenant. But we will be in touch."

Chapter 25

The opening night party was held at New York's venerable show business hangout, Sardi's, just up the street from the Drummond Theater. The celebratory air at the gathering was tempered, to an extent, by the human tragedies surrounding *Knock 'Em Dead*. But the show had gone smoothly, which was reflected in early reviews, and the mood was one of triumph. I'd invited Detectives Hayes and Vasile to the party. I didn't expect them to show up, but Hayes eventually walked in as things were winding down. He was greeted warmly, and a drink was quickly handed him.

"I'm officially off duty," he said, flashing his boyish smile and holding up the glass in a toast: "To *Knock 'Em Dead*, may it live forever on Broadway."

Cast and crew started to file out into the night.

My Cabot Cove friends had gone back to Maine after attending the first night of previews and taking in other Broadway shows.

Linda Amsted said good night and left. She seemed to have gotten over the initial shock of losing people close to her and was in good spirits during the festivities.

Soon, I found myself alone with Lieutenant Henry Hayes as restaurant staff began the cleanup.

"Get you a drink before they take everything away?" he asked.

"Thank you, no. I'm glad you decided to come."

"I'm happy I did. It was Ms. Forrest who sliced your coat."

"She admitted it?"

"Yeah, along with everything else. She was wearing Roy Richardson's coat and hat when she did it. She also wrote those notes to Walpole and Linda Amsted. She's incapable of divorcing fact from fiction, acting from real actions. The DA's office is asking the court to commit her to a psychiatric facility to see if she's fit to stand trial."

"There will be a trial?" I asked. "She's already admitted to the murders."

"Just a formality. The court will have to determine what to do with her. I'm hoping she gets the help she needs."

"I've been wondering, Lieutenant—"

"Henry."

"I've been wondering, Henry, why you arranged for me to go to Roy Richardson's acting class that morning."

He laughed. "My version of a lineup."

"Meaning?"

"We'd been looking at Richardson for over a month as a prime suspect in the serial killings. Frankly, I was convinced he was the killer, and that he was the one who bumped into you on the street and slashed your coat. I thought that by going there and seeing him in person, you might come to the same conclusion. You didn't."

"No, I didn't, nor did I think in those terms about Jenny Forrest."

"It was worth a shot. Your instincts about the Factors were on the money, especially that he was the weak one. I don't think we'd have been able to build a case against her if he hadn't caved in."

"One of the basic motivations for murder," I said.

"What is?"

"Money. Greed. They rank right up there with passion and jealousy."

"Unfortunately, you're right. How's your young bodyguard, Mr. Watson? Enjoying his fame?"

"Oh, he certainly is. Having his picture in the papers here, and back home, is the highlight of his life. Mort Metzger, our sheriff, says he might consider adding Wendell to his force. That would really please him."

"I'm sure it would. When are you going back to Cabot Cove?"

"First thing in the morning. I can't wait."

"Had enough of Broadway for a while?"

"Yes, I think so. Time to face reality again, start work on my next novel, and connect again with the town and people I love. This has been a thrilling experience, but . . ."

"I understand. Next time you're back in New York, give me a call. I'd like to stay in touch."

"You can count on it, Henry. Still glad you became a cop and not an actor?"

"Absolutely, although I just auditioned for a part in a play at my community theater."

"Sounds like fun. What's the part?"

"A cop, of course. It's a murder mystery."

"Any ghosts in your community theater?"

"Not that I know of, but if there is, I'll let you know."

"Well," I said, "as they say, break a leg."

"Or, knock 'em dead."

I smiled. "Yes, that, too."

Based upon advance ticket sales, *Knock 'Em Dead* promised to run on Broadway for years. April Larsen was uniformly praised by reviewers for her performance, with some pointing to the role of

Samantha as propelling the actress to the first rank of Broadway actresses.

A New York freelance journalist contacted me concerning a true crime book he was writing about the Broadway serial killer. I told him what I knew.

Jill and Arnold Factor were convicted of the murders of Harry Schrumm and Vic Righetti and sentenced to life in prison. Jenny was remanded to a psychiatric institution; the prognosis was that she'd never be cured of her insanity and would remain there for the rest of her natural life.

I kept in touch with everyone involved with *Knock 'Em Dead*, especially Detective Henry Hayes and Linda Amsted. I'd learned that Henry was divorced, and thought he and Linda might make a nice couple. The last I heard from either of them, it hadn't happened.

I saw the play a few more times, sitting anonymously in the packed theater and enjoying the audiences' reaction. No matter what had gone before, seeing and hearing my words presented by live actors was a heady experience.

Wendell Watson became a rookie cop in Mort Metzger's police department. I attended his swearing-in ceremony with his mother, Gloria, and shared in her pride.

And I wrote another book.

"Want me to pitch it as another play?" Matt

Miller asked during a phone conversation. "With *Knock 'Em Dead* playing to sold-out audiences, you're a hot Broadway commodity."

"Thanks for the thought, Matt, but please don't. One play in any writer's life is enough."

I left it at that.

Things turn decidedly uncozy
when Jessica travels to
England in the next
Murder, She Wrote mystery:
Gin & Daggers

Just seeing the return address on the envelope filled me with excitement. The letter was from Marjorie Ainsworth, the world's most famous and successful writer of murder mysteries. We'd become friends years ago when I was introduced to her in London by P. D. James, and we'd kept in touch by letter ever since. Not that we communicated with great frequency; I wrote her only two or three times a year, but the number of letters didn't matter. Just being in touch with someone as talented as Marjorie Ainsworth was sufficient for me.

Marjorie Ainsworth's books sold in the millions and were translated into virtually every language on earth. She *defined* the genre, and all murder mysteries written by others were judged against hers.

I couldn't wait to return to England, to spend time with Marjorie, and to join my colleagues at the annual meeting of the International Society of Mystery Writers, or ISMW, as it was commonly referred to. As much as I adopted a toe-in-the-sand response to people in town when they congratulated me on being chosen to be the speaker this year, inside—deep inside—I was proud as could be.

I watched the English countryside slide by— gently rolling hills, idyllic herds of cows grazing on rich grass, fancy sports cars passing us at grand prix speed, tiny villages with women sweeping their sidewalks. How I loved this place, and once again questioned why I'd never followed my instincts to move here. I knew why, of course. Cabot Cove, my home in Maine, was too precious to me to pull up stakes.

Wilfred, the chauffeur, drove with caution until we were abreast of Ainsworth Manor. It stood high on the slope of a hill, gothic in aura, although its architecture was not precisely that. I remembered the last time I approached it and thinking there should be streaks of lightning on a dark scrim behind it. Moviemakers would undoubtedly agree.

We turned onto an access road that was lined with poplar trees and a minute later we were in front of Ainsworth Manor.

"Mrs. Fletcher, how nice to see you again," Jane Portelaine, Marjorie Ainsworth's niece, said to me as I stepped through massive oak doors into a stone-floored foyer.

"It's good to be back," I said, meaning it, although I thought to myself that Jane's presence did not necessarily add to my pleasure. She was obviously a good person, as evidenced by the devotion she'd demonstrated to Marjorie for so many years. The problem with Jane Portelaine was that her severe appearance, coupled with an enigmatic personality, tended to be off-putting, at best.

"I'll check on my aunt now," said Jane. "If she's awake, I'll see if she's well enough to come down."

"Perhaps she'd prefer I come to the bedroom."

"I think not." Jane's long, lanky frame disappeared through a doorway.

A few minutes later she reappeared and said, "She's coming down. Marshall will wheel her."

"Wheel . . . ? I didn't realize she was in a wheelchair."

"Only recently, and not always. It depends on the day. We've had an elevator installed in the rear of the house."

"That sounds like a good idea," I said, a flush of excitement coming over me as I awaited Marjorie's arrival. Then anticipation became reality as the young butler wheeled his mistress through the door and to the center of the study.

"Jessica, I am so sorry to have kept you waiting. Welcome."

I got up and took the hand she offered in both of mine. "How wonderful to see you again, Marjorie. I must say you look a lot better than your last letter indicated you would."

"Bull! I look like the wrath of God, probably because I am closer to him than I have ever been before. But, my dear poppet, thank you for being the kind of friend you have always been."

I took my chair again and closely observed Marjorie Ainsworth. She had grown old and feeble. Her hand, when I took it, seemed nothing but bone and veins covered loosely by leathery skin. Her hair was completely white and appeared not to have been washed and brushed in too long a time. She wore a Black Watch plaid dress that was stained on the bosom. An old, handmade shawl covered her legs. Most telling of her advanced age, however, were her eyes. I don't think I'd ever met anyone in my life whose eyes sparkled with such mischief. Now that sparkle was evident only in fleeting bursts, replaced by dark eyes that had sunk into the bony structure of her face like fresh soil sinking after a heavy rain; dark circles around them gave her skin a puttied appearance. This close scrutiny by me was, at first, upsetting, but then I reminded myself that she was indeed an old woman growing older, and had every right to look it.

The thing that stayed in my mind after the first few minutes was her unkempt condition, and I wondered at the competence and interest of whatever household staff served her these days.

"Jane!" Marjorie shouted in a surprisingly strong and vibrant voice. A moment later Jane Portelaine stood in the doorway. "I'd like a gin," said Marjorie, "and fetch the book for Jessica."

When Jane returned, she carried a glass filled with gin and a copy of *Gin and Daggers*. She handed the drink to Marjorie, the book to me.

"Thank you, I've been looking forward to this ever since it was published." I eagerly opened to the first page and saw that it had been inscribed to me in Marjorie's own handwriting. I was sincerely touched.

"But that's one of Dorothy's enduring traits, Clayton," William Strayhorn, London's most respected book critic, said to Marjorie Ainsworth's American publisher, Clayton Perry. "Read a Dorothy Sayers mystery and you'll always learn something."

"Yes, readers love to learn something while being entertained," Archibald Semple, Marjorie's British publisher, chimed in. "But that doesn't make her better than a writer who doesn't give a tinker's damn about educating readers."

It was Friday night, and we'd been at the dinner table for two hours. The chief topic of discussion throughout the meal had been the relative merits of mystery writers, past and present. The quality of the debates ranged from intently interesting to snide and gossipy. No matter what level they took, however, the presence of the invited guests and their conversation seemed to buoy Marjorie Ainsworth's spirits. She'd spent most of the day with us and, aside from an occasional lapse of concentration and a few brief naps in her wheelchair, had been an active participant.

I'd been more of an observer than an involved member of these spirited discussions. I've always preferred to listen; you learn so much more that way than being compelled to verbalize what you already know. I'd drifted from group to group, enjoying some more than others, laughing at myriad witty lines that erupted from time to time, and generally enjoyed the ambiance of Ainsworth Manor and its weekend visitors.

Marjorie sat at the head of the table. The long day had taken its toll on her; she looked exhausted and was obviously fighting to remain with the group until the last possible minute.

Next to Jane Portelaine sat Bruce Herbert, Marjorie's New York agent. They made an interesting couple. Herbert was as outgoing as Jane was taciturn. It was he who'd proposed the toast at the beginning of dinner:

"To the world's finest crime novelist, Marjorie Ainsworth, who has given millions of people supreme joy through her books, who has set the standard for all writers of the genre. May *Gin and Daggers* be only the latest of your wonderful writings."

"Hear, hear," Archibald Semple had said, his words slurred.

"I have a toast," Marjorie had said.

We'd all looked at her as she raised her glass and said:

> "A thumbprint on the teacup,
> The telltale rigid chin;
> A murder's been committed here,
> Beware the next of kin."

"Bravo," Bruce Herbert said.

"Did you write that?" I asked her.

"Heavens, no, and I have no idea who did."

Now, late in the evening, Count Antonio Zara, Marjorie's brother-in-law, suddenly stood and gave a speech in a heavy accent, after which there was polite applause and Marshall, the servant, supervised the serving of dessert.

"Can we trust this?" Bruce Herbert asked.

Marjorie, who'd been dozing, jerked awake and said in a strong voice, "Trust it? What in heaven's name, do you mean by that?"

Herbert laughed and said, "I've read at least a thousand murder mysteries, Marjorie, in which victims are poisoned by dishes that look like this."

There was laughter at the table. Strayhorn, the critic, said, "I'd debate you on that, Mr. Herbert. I'd say the whiskey decanter had done more people in than syllabub."

"Syllabub?" I said. "What's that?"

Mrs. Horton, the cook, who stood at the door to the kitchen, said, "Whipped cream, sherry, and lemon juice. They used to make it with warm cow's milk."

I looked at my hostess and said lightly, "You haven't decided to poison us all with your syllabub, have you, Marjorie?"

She raised her head and moved her nose, as though a disagreeable odor had reached it. A tiny smile came to her lips as she said, "My dear Jessica, I must be slipping not to have thought of that. What a wonderful way to clear my decks before leaving."

Laughter quickly dissipated as her final words sunk in.

"Whatever do you mean by saying 'leaving'?" asked Archibald Semple.

"You know only too well what I mean, Archie.

I don't expect this dicky body to support me much longer."

Clayton Perry laughed. "You'll probably outlive us all," he said.

"I doubt that," remarked Jane Portelaine, sounding as though she meant it. No one challenged her.

A short while later, Marjorie announced she was going to bed. Her departure broke up the gathering. I then walked upstairs, closed the door behind me, and prepared for bed.

I sat bolt upright. I didn't know what time it was. Had I been asleep ten minutes, an hour, four hours?

It was a sound that had awakened me, and it seemed to come from Marjorie's room, next to mine. How to describe it? A cry for help? Not really. Sounds from someone engaged in a struggle? More like it, but hardly accurate. Whatever it was, it had been loud enough to awaken me and sinister enough to cause me to get out of bed, slip into my robe and slippers, and open my door.

I entered the hallway, stepping gingerly as the ancient floorboards creaked beneath my feet, a sound I hadn't heard since awakening.

I placed my fingertips against Marjorie's door and pushed. It was heavy and did not swing open, and had to be pushed more. I did that and peered into the room. Marjorie's bed was king-size and covered with a canopy. The room was dark except for a sharp shaft of moonlight that poured through an opening in the drapes. It was perfectly aimed, as though a theater lighting technician had highlighted a section of a stage where major action would occur.

I stepped over the threshold and walked to the side of the bed, like a moth drawn to a summer candle. A whole arsenal of grotesque sounds rose up inside me, but stopped at my throat—sounds of protest, of outrage, of shock and horror. Yet not a sound came from me as I looked down at the body of Marjorie Ainsworth, the grande dame of murder mystery fiction, sprawled on her back, arms and legs flung out, a long dagger protruding from her chest like a graveyard marker.

All I managed to say—and it was in a whisper—was "Oh my God." As I turned to leave, my slippered foot hit a metal object and propelled it under the bed. I didn't stop to see what it was.

I returned to the hallway and stood at the railing, my hands gripping it as I drew a deep breath to fill my lungs. I shouted, "Help! Please come quickly! There's been a murder!"